WHERE WE ONCE BELONGED

WHERE WE ONCE BELONGED

SIA FIGIEL

 KAYA

Kaya Press edition, 1999
Third printing, 2007
Originally published by Pasifika Press, New Zealand
Printed in Canada

Kaya Press
an imprint of Muae Publishing, Inc.
http://www.kaya.com

Cover design by John Kunichika
Book design by Juliana Koo

Distributed by DAP/Distributed Art Publishers
155 Avenue of the Americas, 2nd Floor
New York, NY 10013
(800) 338-BOOK http://www.artbook.com

ISBN: 1-885030-27-4
ISBN 13: 978-1-885030-27-6
Library of Congress Catalog Card Number 99-91103

The publication of this book was made possible in part by the generous support of the
New York State Council on the Arts, a state agency, Soo Kyung Kim, Wook Hun and
Sun Hee Koo, Edward Lin, Paul H. Smith, Eileen Tabios and Tom Pollack, Ronald and
Susan Yanagihara, Hong Yung and Whakyung Lee, Minya Oh, and many others.

For the women
(who are always a step ahead)
and the girls
(who know everything there is to know)

BUZZING EVERYWHERE

When I saw the insides of a woman's vagina for the first time I was not alone. I was with Lili and Moa. Lili's name was Maʻalili, but everyone called her Lili. Moa's name was Moamoalulu, but everyone called her Moa. Lili was seventeen and Moa was sixteen. They were older than me. They were already menstruating.

Lili got it when she was eleven, which is a record in Malaefou history. Moa got it when she was thirteen…and couldn't stop bragging about the fact that not only did she get it at thirteen, which was only two years after the record, but that most important of all, she got it before me.

Which meant I had to give her half my earnings from the coke bottles we all sold at Faamelea's.

I had lost the bet.

I was the last in our circle to catch the moon sickness.

—

To all Malaefou teenagers, girls and boys, we were Charlie's Angels. Everyone who knew us called us by our TV names—

Kelly, Sabrina, and Jill. As is the custom in Malaefou, girls went around in groups. Some were glued to their own cousins. Others, like Lili, Moa, and me, came from different households.

Sometimes a girl would be a loner. Like Makaoleafi—eye of the fire—who not only was the goodest girl in the whole of Malaefou, but also the meanest and the strongest.

She spent most of her time at the faifeau's house serving matai on Sundays. Laulau le sua. She knew the faalupega o Malaefou backwards, plus all the polite forms of chicken, pig, and other food. She proudly said them out loud enough for those of us who didn't know and struggled always to remember.

She never tried a cigarette—that is, no adult had ever seen or heard of her smoking. Didn't own a pair of pants—that is, she never wore one in Malaefou. And no stories ever lead to her— that is to say, she was not a faikakala.

Our own mothers would say, 'She is *such* a good girl. I wish she were my daughter.'

Girls would say, 'She's a snake in disguise.'

A disguise we all knew too well. A disguise we ourselves used from time to time.

Afi was the epitome of a Malaefou young lady. And because of this she was safe...safe to do anything...safe to be a bad girl at nights and no one suspected.

Boys paid her money just to smell her panties. Grown men paid her money, too, just to smell her panties and bra. Some were even allowed to smell her panties while she was menstruating...if she was in the mood for it.

She made a boy cry one day, with a slap on the face and an elbow to his stomach, for beating up her older brother, Semisi.

She was only ten and in Standard Four. He was thirteen and sitting the national exams.

She pulled Miss Cunningham's hair one day at school after Miss Cunningham gave her an F in Maths, ripped up the suspension note and spent her days at the movies or the market. She warned anyone against telling her parents about it. She would rearrange their faces if she ever found out. She was twelve.

When we talked about Afi we whispered. We whispered and whispered. And when she would see us she would say, 'If I find out you're whispering about me, I'm gonna break your face! Understand?'

We whispered anyway. Anyway. In our very invisible voices. Loud enough for ants and snails and beer bottles to hear.

In our circle we whispered about Afi being a pau'elo. Her skin stank because she never took showers. And she wore the same dress Salu, her sister, wore on Mondays and Thursdays. It was never washed and you could smell it. She was practically afraid of water, practically afraid of soap. Like a flying fox hanging from a cave—from a cave—so was her scent. She smelled of bats…a hundred bats put together. Bats lived in her armpits, in the crotch of her panties.

'Faipepea!' we would yell out in our beer-bottle voices.

'Afi, faipepea! Pa'uelo! Le kaelea!' we whispered and whispered.

Afi always caught Moa, whose voice took on visible form on rare moments. And Afi would pull her hair, scratch her face, throw stones at her legs…or called Max and Rum on her—Max and Rum being the fiercest dogs in the whole of Malaefou—while Lili and I ran and ran, to the mango tree, to the church, to the pigsty where we all met later and talked some more about

Afi...and how one day we were gonna make her pay.

In all our whisperings, and in all our yelling and our insulting her scent, it almost sounded like we were praising her...which perhaps we were, but never quite wanted to admit to. Even as we yelled out these insults in our ant voices, we knew deep down that we were envious and jealous...and we hated it and despised it. Why did she have to be so-so sure of herself? So-so good. And so-so strong? And so-so *smelly*?

Unlike us who were clean-clean always. And proud, too, of the fact that we saved lunch money to smell of Wella Apple Shampoo...which in turn led to none of the boys or men asking us if they could smell *our* panties...let alone our bras.

'You're *too* clean,' the boys and men would say.

'Too clean. You are too clean,' they would say.

When boys and men said to us, 'You're too clean. You are too clean,' I was confused for days. Why would they want to smell someone's panties and bras when that someone smelled of a bat, a dog, a toilet? And why weren't they attracted to the scent of apples on our skin?

That whole week Moa and I stopped taking showers. We deliberately hugged Whiskey. Which our cousins could not understand. We both hated dogs. We even put baby piss in our hair and had farting competitions. Still boys and men found us too clean. We gave up after three days. Utterly frustrated! Hating Afi more and more.

We hated and despised Afi not only because she had the smell, or that she was the strongest girl in the whole of Malaefou...and meanest...but worse.

Because despite all this—or rather, in spite of all this—she

4

remained a good girl…a good girl in the eye of everyone.

I suppose we, too, wanted to be good girls. And we were constantly disappointed at our mothers for saying that we were not. We were in-betweens…that is to say we were not completely good and we were not completely bad.

To be in-betweens meant that we went to church: twice on Sundays and once during the fogo a kiakogo on Wednesdays—which we attended as assistants and found utterly dull since there were no boys around…with the exception of Lealofi, the faifeau's son, who played the piano. But who wanted *him*?

During this dullest of all chores we were supposed to fetch things for the kiakogo—may it be bibles, or hymn books, or papers, or glasses of water, or hymn books some more—things which took up a whole two hours of our lives on Wednesdays and were followed immediately by prayers at the fale o le faifeau in the evenings.

We never missed a meeting of the Aufaipese, or of the Aukalavou, or of the Au a Keine. We were *always* at the Aoga a le Faifeau *and* the Aoga Aso Sa, passed sewing tests, learned our lines for White Sunday, helped the faletua a le faifeau weed the garden around their house, helped the Women's Committee dry pandanus leaves, helped our own mothers dry pandanus leaves, did the washing of clothes and dishes, cooked saka, ironed Sunday clothes—which was expected of us anyway. Yet despite all this goodness we were not good—in-betweens only. We were in-betweens because we loved laughing, and laughed and laughed at the slightest things.

When Elia, a matai, was playing volleyball. And jumped up to spike the ball. And his lavalava fell. And he was not wearing underwears. We laughed.

We laughed when Mu's father wanted to borrow money from his palagi boss and told the palagi he needed it for Mu's funeral …even though Mu was the healthiest of all his children.

We laughed whenever Sugar Shirley, the fa'afafige, walked around Malaefou with nothing but Tausi's panties and bra stuffed with coconuts.

These incidents filled our days with butterflies and grasshoppers. They were labelled however by the village women—and our own mothers, especially—as aka kauvala'au, aka kaukala'ikiki, aka fia fai kage, aka a'amu, pa'umumuku…and so on. What were we supposed to do to reverse the verdict that we were only in-betweens? And why was it so important for us to be 'good'?

———

The answer was revealed to us one evening after watching an episode of *Charlie's Angels*.

Lili was Kelly. She had the best haircut, black hair (clean of uku), blue eyes (big-big), breasts (big-big), pretty legs (with no sores blasted all around them). She always carried a gun in her purse.

I was Jill and I had blonde hair, blue eyes (too), *always* wore pink lipstick, sunglasses, jeans, and had an eighteen-inch waist. Moa was Sabrina. She looked part-Chinese, straight black hair, never wore a dress, and was perhaps the cleverest of the three of us. She was the one that came up with the idea of exposing the eye of the fire. We jokingly referred to Mr Brown as Charlie.

Mr Brown was a palagi and worked for the Bank of Western Samoa. Lili told us he was a Communist.

'Ei! What's a Communist do?'

'He counts money.'

'Oh...!'

Mr Brown the Communist—which Afi later corrected to Economist (but we didn't care about it anyway, because we didn't know the difference between Communist and Economist)—lived on the edge of our village where the mango trees with fruit grew, where boys kissed girls in the dark, where that old nun died.

He lived by himself. He had a dog named Dingo.

Mr Brown knew about Jesus, but was not a church-goer. His favourite words were 'fucking-fucking-Jesus-Christ.' Mr Brown never called Lili, Lili. He always called her Sheila...*my* Sheila... my Samoan Sheila.

Lili washed Mr Brown's clothes, ironed Mr Brown's clothes, polished his shoes, cleaned his flushing toilet, cooked dinner for him...she was just like a wife. Lili was Mr Brown's keigefaigalue-ga. And Moa and I were the only girls allowed to go into Mr Brown's house when Mr Brown was not there.

When Mr Brown was not there Lili would show us all the rooms in Mr Brown's house.

'This is where he sleeps. He sleeps on this bed. This other bed is for Dingo. This is where he keeps his shoes. He has eight pairs, each one for a special occasion. Sometimes he tells me to polish a pair and he'll wear them throughout the whole week. Sometimes he gives old pairs to clerks at the bank. That's where he keeps his books. A lot, eh?'

'Ei! Do you think he's read all of them?'

'Who cares if he has?'

'This is where he keeps the towels and the sheets and pillowcases. This is where he keeps the soap and Ajax and mop and brooms. This is where he keeps the machete and the rakes and the....'

'Where does Mr Brown keep the food?'

Lili stopped what she was saying and looked at us. She knew that that was the only reason Moa and I visited her, and it was written so blatantly all over our faces. She continued with her description of the house as if she didn't hear the food question. And that's when Moa started coughing and coughing...and I joined in, hinting that we didn't care much about the house and that we would really like her to answer our little question.

Try as we might Lili did not pay much attention to our coughing. So Moa said something like she knew of someone who had the eye for her...and that she would only reveal his name when we were shown where the food was. Lili stopped suddenly, turned around, and ran out of the house. 'What's that supposed to mean?' I wanted to ask. But then we heard thunder and more thunder...and rain was pissing on the tin-roof. We saw Lili pulling Mr Brown's clothes from the wire.

There was a vase of teuila on the table there in the middle of the kitchen.

'Ei! Why do you think palagis put flowers in their houses? Aren't there enough flowers outside to look at?'

'Who cares?' I said, trying to avoid any further questions...all I wanted was food.

'Maybe because they don't go to church on Sundays, so they try to make their houses look like one. Or maybe he can't afford to buy real flowers. You know, *plastic* flowers—what a shame!'

There were pictures of Mr Brown and Dingo smiling, Dingo

jumping, Dingo jumping again, Mr Brown eating an ice cream …stuck onto the refrigerator under Bank of Western Samoa magnets.

'Ei! Do you think he has any ice cream in the icebox?' Moa whispered. 'It's not like he's gonna notice if we take one or two scoops out, e?'

'He doesn't have any ice cream, you two.' Lili's voice flew from her mouth like cricket balls, hitting us both on the faces. She stood there on the steps of the house, hands full of clothes, dripping wet.

'Shit! I knew you would be up to something! Besides, even if he did have ice cream, you are not getting any. He never keeps ice cream in the icebox anyway. Only when guests come. Oh shit, don't look at me like that. I hate it when you do that. Okay, I suppose you could look around while I dry myself. I'll take out some leftovers when I come back. But remember, no funny business…okay?'

We opened the icebox anyway. Just to make sure there wasn't any ice cream stacked somewhere in the bottom. None. We opened the cupboard too. Opened the drawers to the cupboard. Opened the stove. Opened the cupboards again…and that's when I spotted a box of cornflakes sitting high up on the top level of the cupboard.

I had never seen cornflakes in real life. I'd always seen them on TV. A woman pouring milk into a bowl of cornflakes. A man smiling at the woman. The woman smiling at a boy. The boy smiling at a girl. The girl smiling at a big dog. Happy music everywhere. Cornflakes made palagi people happy. I wanted to see what it could do to Moa and me.

'No, Alofa!' said Lili. Rushing into the kitchen. 'That's a new box. You shouldn't open it! Do you want me to get fired, e?'

'Could I just touch it then?'

Just to say I've touched a box of cornflakes?

As I reached up to touch the box, a magazine fell from the cupboard. It must have been folded next to the cornflakes and the tall bottle of sugar. Down came the magazine. It fell open right on my feet. Naked women were all over the pages.

'Ei…! What's *this?*'

'What's what?' asked Lili back, in a very surprised/embarrassed voice. 'I've never seen it before.'

'Let me have a look,' said Moa, snatching the magazine away from my hands, her mouth wide open when she saw the cover-page. 'You've been working here now for Mr Brown for six months. And Mr Brown has *never* shown you *any* of this before?'

Lili looked outside then back inside again, pretending to not be embarrassed with Moa's question. Everyone in the village was talking about her and Mr Brown. They were saying that the word keigefaigaluega was only a front for what Lili really did for Mr Brown. Women were constantly whispering about her.

'I bet she cleans more than just house.'

'Do you really think they've already done "it"?'

'Stay away from her.'

'She's not a girl anymore.'

'She's a bloody woman and she's bad.'

'Who wears makeup to church, e?'

'Who doesn't wear a bra to church?'

'She even smokes.'

'And uses bad language.'

10

'That mother of her's should wash her mouth with Omo.'

'And don't even mention the father.'

'That's where she gets it from.'

'She's a bad influence on you girls.'

'Stay away from her.'

'Stay away…'

'Away…'

Moa and I knew otherwise. We knew much more about her than anyone else—besides her own father, Iosua. It's true…but that's another story. And with this knowledge in mind I wanted to bite off Moa's head. For being so stupid as to say what she did.

To change the awkwardness of the situation I quickly asked, 'Do you think we should look at it?'

'I'm hungry, Alofa,' said Moa, in her silly voice which escapes her mouth for no other reason other than to exercise her jaws.

'I don't want to look at anything,' she added. 'I just want some food and something to drink so I can hurry home and do my homework.'

'Do your *what?* In broad daylight? Are you out of your mind?'

'Oh, shut up, Alofa…and hurry up with your stupid magazine.'

'*You* wanna see it just as much as I do, you selfish little…'

'Stop it you two! Just stop it! You're both making me sick with your whiny little voices. Just open the damn thing, look at it, and go home, okay?

We had never seen that part of our bodies so close up before. We never knew what was behind all the hair. I was the last to grow hair (and breasts). This I knew because Lili used to say that I was bald, and that if I didn't stop eating sugarcane I would never grow hair…never grow breasts.

'Sugarcane makes your body weak, Alofa. Weak because sugarcane is sweet and you are sour…an "in-between." You need to be *completely* sour to be a woman.'

'What is *that* supposed to mean?' I asked, but no one heard. No one wanted to hear. This while we showered naked at Moa's fale one evening.

Moa's 'aiga were the only ones who had a paipa surrounded with tin. Moa's father decided one day to surround the shower with tin. Makaaiku, the village pervert, and Iosua, Lili's father, were caught again—for the hundredth time—spying on Laulii's daughters and once or twice on his wife. Since then the tin went up, and I took all my showers at Moa's paipa.

The women in the magazine were very happy-looking…but not cornflake happy. Some were smiling a lot. Others looked like they wanted to pick fights. Some were touching their breasts with the tips of their claws. Others did not. Some were touching their vaginas with the tips of their claws. Others did not. Some spread their legs apart as if waiting for a doctor. Others did not. Some wore bras without panties. Others wore panties without bras. Some of the panties had holes in the crotch. Others had panties with such thin material that anyone could see all their hair.

'That's the idea isn't it, Alofa?'

'What did you say?'

'I said… Oh, forget it! You'll never learn.'

Suddenly my panties were wet in the crotch…and that had never happened before. My heart was beating-beating-beating also. I was afraid of what was happening, and I was hoping, too, that Lili and Moa's crotches were also wet.

'Ei! O susu le maga o lua ofuvae?' I wanted to ask.

Lili was laughing and laughing. She mustn't have heard my question clearly, so I asked again in my snail-voice.

'Are your crotches wet?'

I must have looked so strange, so serious when I said this, because Moa and Lili stopped their laughing immediately.

Moa said to me in her calmest voice, 'What's wrong with you? What's wrong with you? Are you gonna tell on us?'

Because I was the youngest, and because the youngest is always the eyes and ears of the 'aiga or of the faletua a le faifeau, Moa asked me again.

'Are you gonna *tell* on us?'

I had not thought of telling anyone anything. My crotch was just suddenly wet. I wanted to know why…and I wanted to know whether or not Lili and Moa felt the same sensations in their panties.

Moa (whispering-whispering-whispering), 'You're not gonna tell on us are you?'

This time I didn't hear her. I must have been dead because Moa had to practically yell—a second, or third, or tenth time—to get me to hear her.

'No, I won't tell. I swear. I won't tell.'

'Swear to God!' they yelled out. 'Kauko i luma o le Akua!'

'Swear on your father's name!'

'But he can't even see us! He's at work!'

'Swear! Kauko i luma o Filiga!'

Lili (laughing this time), 'Swear on your namesake Alofa's grave!'

'Eat shit!'

'Swear to God again…and mean it!'

I swore to Lili and Moa that I would not tell anyone about us watching women touch their fucking-fucking-Jesus-Christ vaginas!

'Satisfied?'

They busted out laughing. They laughed some more and some more, until suddenly Moa stopped and looked at us as if she had just seen Lafoga or Filiga or Fauakafe.

'What is it?'

'I have an idea.'

Whenever Moa had an idea I became nervous. Most of her ideas got us into fist fights, mouth fights, and sometimes under Filiga's wrath. She snatched the magazine from my hands, lifted her shirt up (exposing her very flat chest) and ran out of the house. The last thing we saw was her laugh, which was always the loudest, following her into Malaefou...accompanied by T–R–O–U–B–L–E.

—

The rest of the day I spent trying to forget those women. Trying to forget the way they smiled. I tried to forget the way their tongues played on their lips. Tried to forget-forget-forget. But each time I remembered them my crotch would get wet.

'Something wrong with you, Alofa?' my cousin Sisifo asked me after prayer that evening.

'Why do you ask?'

'You didn't begin the aftersong for the lotu.'

'I have a test tomorrow.'

'Oh, you don't know then do you?'

'Don't know about what?'

'You don't know about Makaoleafi?'

'What about Makaoleafi? What has she done this time? Has she married an a'oa'o? Is she pregnant through virginal conception? Or was she visited by angels in the middle of a shit?'

'Her mother sent her to Filiga this afternoon…beaten up bad. She has a black eye and a shaved head. Filemu found a dirty magazine in her schoolbag.'

—

I avoided seeing Moa that night. I avoided seeing Lili. I avoided eye contact with anyone at the table. I sat there looking at the food—taro and bananas in coconut milk with tuna and supa keli. This was a delicacy. A meal fit only for Tausi and the elders of the fale. I knew exactly why it was sitting on my plate.

The supa keli stared at me and I stared back at it—at them. Worms they were, swimming in the milk of the coconut.

The voices around the table became louder and louder, filled with sinister whisperings and low laughter.

'And all this time we thought she was an angel!'

'Like I always said, don't judge a koko alaisa until you taste it—ha!'

'Ka igo igo e.'

'I suppose our Alofa is not that bad after all—despite her cheekiness. At least she only laughs.'

'Ha, ha!' laughed the worms on my plate. 'Go ahead Alofa. Give us one now. We wanna hear, too, how beautifully you can sing.'

I grabbed the plate and threw it on the floor. It made a loud sound. Whiskey ran from his post and started licking the tin.

'Kick that dog away from there!'

'Ei, ua e valea?'

'Aikae…and pick that all up before the dog eats it, you ungrateful girl. There's people hungry all over kua back and Savai'i, and here she is throwing tuna and supa keli away as if…as if…'

'…she wants to taste Filiga's talking stick.'

'She wants to be like Afi.'

'Give her a little taste of…'

—

When the lights went out that night I died with them. I died to forget. I died to escape. For I knew the rules to Malaefou politics too well. E kaui le maka i le maka—this has never failed.

When Sila, a girl of fourteen, called Fa'avevesi's mother a whore who was screwing all the aumaga of Malaefou, war was waged and Sila's mother was taken to Motootua Hospital. She couldn't see straight for days.

When Mafatia beat Ioelu's head with a homebrew bottle and told everyone there that Fautua, Ioelu's father, was a thief who stole pigs from their family's sty, war was waged and all the taule'ale'a of Ioelu's family set a lama for any of Mafatia's family caught outside of Malaefou. Lumana'i, one of Mafatia's brothers, was caught and tied up like a pig with afa, and wrapped in a taro-sack and thrown into the sea. This after he was beaten with fists and sticks and stones. He was found, luckily, by Manuao the fisherman who brought him to land and called out to Mu's 'aiga's taxi, who drove the bleeding-and-nearly-dying (from lack of oxygen) Lumana'i to Motootua National Hospital.

'What was Afi thinking?' I asked myself.

Did she even know that it was us?

Was she already planning to wage war?

Before I could find an answer I was already dead, my fingers travelling like clouds down to the darkness of my hair…and I was floating then, floating-floating above clouds, float gently, float gently into sleep…floating-floating into death…

—

People see surfaces only, and that's all. They don't care to look under tables, or under mats, or in a book, or bite a fruit. They like admiring these things, admiring the way things look only on the outside. On the outside, that is on the surface of a table, everything is beautiful. Everything would be the tablecloth, the tablecloth decorated with little red roses…or perhaps a white house with blue windows on the top floor and a little white fence, sealing the garden and the house in. Everyone would adore this tablecloth, and see it only and say, 'That's such a beautiful table! How marvellous!'

But that wasn't the table. That was the tablecloth! You haven't seen the table—the table hidden under the tablecloth. What do you know then of this table? Is it made out of wood completely, or is made out of metal or paper? How do you know then that it's a table? After all, it could be a big paper box covered with the tablecloth to make it look like a table.

This same principle is applicable to human beings…or people, as they are commonly known. People prefer to see the tablecloths of other people, that is, how they look, how their bodies look, how their clothes look, how their purses look, etc., etc. People define other people as good or bad, or clever or stupid, or clever or bad—depending on the surface only…in essence, their table-cloths.

In my village, if a girl could recite the entire fa'alupega of Malaefou, serve matai on Sunday, know also the polite forms for chicken and pig, she was good, she was admired, she was worshipped even.

Lili, my friend, for example, is known to everyone in Malaefou as the paumuku. Everyone thinks she sleeps with sailors and Korean fishing men from American Samoa. Everyone thinks she sleeps with anything that moves…and that she does 'it' with Mr Brown…and that she's a slut. We are warned constantly of her. We are warned constantly against her…as if she were a pest, as if she was the animal on one of those typical warning signs on the fences of people's houses or nailed to a tree:

Warning—Dog Bites. Enter At Own Risk.

Which is my next point: is there more than one surface to a human being?

The outside surface?

And the inside?

And the inside?

The inside surface is hard to see at first glance. I know. Unlike a table—with its cotton tablecloth, or plastic tablecloth that could be easily removed to discover if the table was made out of wood, or out of metal or paper—the inside of a people is hard to get to simply because there are so many different layers. Every time you think you've taken one layer off, another one appears…and appears…and keeps appearing. Until you finally give up. You say, 'Enough of this! Enough of layers. I'm sick and tired of layers! I don't want to see or discover a new one!'

This was the same feeling I thought I had before Moa planted the magazine of those women in Makaoleafi's schoolbag. I couldn't go to sleep because I was thinking about that constantly. I was thinking and thinking of Afi being sent to Filiga to be beaten, questioned over and over as if she was a criminal. And how she refused to say anything. And how her eyes were all black, and her hair cut short and shaved to further humiliate her. And how she missed school for two days because she couldn't move.

And it was all our fault—my fault.

The shock of it all is that I had been expecting war that whole week. I had really armed myself each time I left the house, trying to avoid Afi's house, cousins, and dogs. Each time I stepped out of the house I took at least four good-sized stones in my pockets, just in case. But I was never provoked to use them, not once.

I remember the first time I saw Afi and that was two weeks after the beating. It was on a Tuesday afternoon. I had come home by bus that day and we were all squeezed in together, all of us schoolgirls. Laughing-laughing about the bus driver, the netball game with Leififi, and the bus driver (again) who wiggled his tongue in the mirror every time one of us looked at him.

Someone rang the stop at our village and got out. I got out, too. Suddenly I was next to a cave of bats. They attacked my eyes. They attacked my teeth. They attacked my nose. The bats forced their way up my nostrils, all the way to my brain. And I found myself running in the forest. I was running and running, and I came upon Afi. And Afi was standing there too in the forest, her arms stretching to the sky.

Birds flew out of her belly button. Bees and ants and other small insects danced between her fingers, in her armpits, on her toes. Moist, too, was the fern on her nipples, on her neck. And a small river fell from the triangle of her pubic hair.

Yes, there I was suddenly, confronted with Afi's scent. She now smelled of gardenia…even though it was not gardenia season.

And I asked myself, 'Is *that* why boys and men wanted to look at her brown panties and bra? Because they found the gardenia season there, all year round? In the brownness of her crotch? In the bush of her armpits? Gardenia which we girls mistook for bats and lack of soap?'

Afi looked me straight in the eyes and I looked down (so embarrassed). I was all alone then. No Moa next to me. No Lili. Not a single rock in my pockets. It was just the two of us.

She said 'I'm sorry' to me as if *I* was the one beaten up.

'I'm sorry, Alofa' is all she said to me and then she got up and walked away.

'What is this supposed to mean?' I asked myself. 'Why didn't Afi declare war on us? On *me*? She could have easily pulled my hair or scratched my eyes. After all, she *was* the strongest girl in the whole of Malaefou…and I was all alone, anyway. Why?'

'Maybe she was tired that day,' I whispered to myself. 'Maybe she had a test or something more important to attend to and she thought I was just another girl. Or maybe it is all part of being a people with not only a surface but many layers.'

You think, or rather you are convinced so much, that you know the surface and that you know some of the layers, but then you come to the end and you are surprised…shocked even.

Instead of finding a polluted dump in the middle of the night—which is what you expected all along—you come to a river. And there are prawns eating moons—and bees, too, buzzing...everywhere.

IN THE WIND, IN THE DARK

Sometimes in the evenings—when we got bored and there was nothing else to do, and there was no Aufaipese, or Aukalavou, or Au a keine, or Bingo for that matter, or we'd already exhausted the subject of boys, bad girls, pregnancies, food, affairs, etc., and there was nothing good on TV—we counted and recounted all our relatives, over and over.

This we did at nights, when the moon was awake and pulu leaves were awake, and flying foxes were awake, too…squeaking-squeaking in the middle of the malae. And all of us girls would sit in a circle there, too, in the malae—our circle; the 'girl circle,' as the boys called it. They whistled and laughed, too, clapping their hands or calling out our names.

'I love Moa!'

'I love Sisila!

'I'm gonna marry you, Alofa, when I grow up. Ha, ha!'

All of which we ignored…too busy talking about ourselves or boys from other villages.

We would sit there and sing songs and dance, facing the government road. Recounting all our relatives again, not able to forgive ourselves if we woke up the next day and we remembered someone we had forgotten the night before. Downright sinful!

For we knew everyone in our village, *everyone.* All the way from the oldest to the newest born. From the angelic to the not-so-angelic...to sleepwalkers...to thieves...to lovers...to the faithful...to lovers again...and relatives again, too. We knew them all, repeating their names over and over to make sure we didn't leave anyone out—which happened ninety-eight percent of the time. Counting, too, the many people named after a certain name.

There were ten Savalis in our village. There were six Tanielus. Four Elegis. Four Fales. Two Sisilas. Two Efus. Two Iosuas. Ten families whose sons are named after their fathers and had this symbol at the end of their names: 'II.'

We knew *everyone.* Of course we did! We're girls...and girls knew everything there was to know in Malaefou. (Besides women who were always a step or two ahead of us.)

When Pua was sent to New Zealand three years ago, everyone thought she was on a government scholarship. Of course, everyone believed it! After all Pua was the only girl from here to attend Samoa High School, and came second place in Form Three and was a prefect in Form Four...who was the only daughter of Malaefou to skip Lower Fifth.

Who would have suspected that she was three months pregnant? And that she had done it with Mr Maseligo, who was twenty-three years older than her, and had eight children from three different wives, who all lived around him in Lalovaea—in not so much harmony—in their very separate houses and with their very separate children, who all played with each other, calling each other their best friends?

And he was so so ugly! Who would even look at him twice? Not even Siniva, the fool of Malaefou, I'm sure. There was absolutely *nothing* to look at...even if he was the best Maths teacher at S.C. and the most fierce disciplinarian—known among students as Faipapa'u—who wasn't circumcised and used a hose to give hidings to anyone not knowing the root of 49 or other. Is there a correlation?

Big ears. Small eyes. No lips. Short legs. And a mole the size of parliament building at Mulinu'u founded between his nose and upper lip.

'Yuk!' we all went.

'Yuk!'

And:

'Change the subject someone. *Pleeease!*'

'Okay, let's talk about weddings! About *my* wedding,' said Moa. 'When I get married I want twelve bridesmaids, six on each side with pink lacey dresses and pink high heels...and a pink cake, too. A pink cake, too. With twenty—no, twenty-five floors, and twenty cars, too...and five hundred guests, dressed up in Sunday best, at the Tusitala Hotel. No, make that Aggie Grey's.'

'And who'll be the groom?'

Yes, who'll be the groom? Sylvester Stallone? Chuck Norris? Or Bruce Lee? Oh! the choices! The choices!

'What about Vikale?' the boys yelled out in wicked laughter. 'Or Stupo? Moa's gonna marry Stupo! Ha! Stupo with the wooden leg and no front teeth and...'

'Stop it!' said Moa. 'You're just jealous, just jealous.... That Stupo is more handsome than any of you flies put together. There!'

And we all roared in laughter—high-pitched laughter which the boys despised—silencing them until we were sprayed suddenly with pebbles and threats.

'We're *never* gonna ask you to play iga vea with us.'

'Good,' we yelled back, knowing full well that it's not half as much fun when they play alone and that they'll ask us back anyway. So we went on with our laughter, swirling in our circle.

'Hey, what about Pili?' says Sisifo.

'Pili the thief?'

'Let's talk about Pili. You tell it, Moa.'

'I just told about my wedding!'

'You tell it then, Fale.'

'Tell it, Fale…and don't miss a single part out.'

'Oh, this is good! This is really really good. Ready?'

Pili stole apples, and ketchup, and saimin, and Jack Daniel's, too, from an open container at the wharf…and faked suicide. When the nightwatcher caught him he poured ketchup all over his head, cracked the top of an empty Vailima bottle and held it in his hand until the poor nightwatcher fled for help.

And Pili picked up his sack of apples, and ketchup, and saimin, and Jack Daniel's, and ran all the way home…only to be caught by Iosua II—the strongest and fastest man in the *whole* of Malaefou, known for rearranging faces due to his temper, and the best hooker in the whole of Rugby League. He was making out with the not-so-angelic Fa'amaoni, the pastor's middle daughter, under the pastor's ulu. Iosua II stopped Pili and told him to give him a bottle of ketchup, a few saimin, two apples for his daughter… and a bottle of Jack Daniel's, too. No one would know about the incident. That was his word.

Pili protested. Protested and protested, wiping the remaining ketchup off the top of his head. He protested some more, even though he knew his chances were nil to nil.

'Leave my stuff alone,' he said. 'I just came back from Emilio's.'

'He's still open for late-night customers. Ask him tomorrow!' said Pili in his very shaky voice.

Upon which time Iosua lost respect...or rather politeness... grabbed the sack, took out what he wanted, and went back to doing what he was doing to Fa'amaoni.

Upon which time Pili yelled out, 'I'm gonna tell you on your wife anyway!'

...and fled.

Iosua did not like Pili's talk—talk about Pele, who's at home with their five children and sick cat, probably asleep...or at Mu's watching *Days*.... In which case he ran after Pili, who had just crossed the church fence, pulled at his lavalava—that fell off instantly—and Pili stood there, naked in front of church and God to see.

And Iosua didn't have to say anything to Pili...because Pili *volunteered* another four apples, seven packages of saimin, another bottle of Jack Daniel's and the half empty bottle of ketchup he had used to fake his own suicide, in return for Iosua's promise not to rearrange his face—broken only when Fa'amaoni, the pastor's daughter, was caught drunk (naked, too) under the ulu the next morning and the whole of Malaefou knew about it...knew about where the booze came from too. Most people thought this was funny, and congratulated Pili on fooling the nightwatcher. They knew, too, about why Fa'amaoni was naked...this after Pili's detailed confession (feeling so sure that everyone was on his side).

Then Pele left Malaefou with the kids, and all the food, and the tape recorder from Australia, and the electric saw, and sick cat. And *that's* when Iosua broke his promise and did serious harm to Pili, who was taken to Motootua and stayed there for a week. After which time everyone called him 'Jack' and Iosua 'Daniels.'

—

Isn't that the best...*ever?*

'That's *not* the best,' says Salala, the biggest girl in Malaefou... and the serious-est. The only girl strong enough to beat up Afi the bully if she wanted to.

'That's not the best,' she said. 'It isn't. How can you say it is?'

'How can you *not* say it is?' asked Moa boldly, well aware that she was much lighter than Salala and could speed away if trouble ever arose.

'Nothing is better than counting relatives,' says Salala again, as if she had not heard Moa. 'Nothing is better than counting relatives...and their whereabouts, and belongings. *Nothing.* Don't you agree?'

She was right. For a while there we were all silenced. Salala was right. And we all agreed...and agreed. Nothing is better than counting relatives...besides a good kung-fu movie. But that's different altogether. We loved counting relatives. We loved doing it the most. And we did it over and over. And it was always clear at the end of each night that Mulimuli—or Mu, when someone showed affection, or Muli, when not—had the biggest 'aiga *ever.* They were the richest, too.

Mu's 'aiga had a falepapalagi with real chairs from Folasi in

New Zealand, which no one was allowed to sit on and which were covered still with the plastic they were bought in. And they were used only by Lafoga the pastor, visiting matai, or lost palagis.

The chairs were dusted every morning by Mu and the other girls of their 'aiga, who brought out soap and rags and pails of water and scrubbed. We were left standing outside, envious... wishing, too, we had that chore. We didn't have chairs. Chairs covered with plastic, anyway.

Two coloured TVs. Mu's family had two coloured TVs—one on the first floor of the fale, and the other on the second floor in Pola and Lalolagi's room—and all the kids and some adults went there to watch *Little House on the Prairie, Charlie's Angels,* and *Dallas.*

Plus a video machine, too...with *Rambo,* and Mickey Mouse, and men and women without clothes (which Sale and the boys watched when everyone else was asleep).

An electric fan.

Pictures of Jesus Christ with one finger pointing to the leak in the roof—two hung on the first floor, and another made of velvet (red velvet) hung in the living room on the second floor, next to the large poster of Elvis with a red lei around his neck in Aloha attire, singing *Blue Hawaii* on a bridge (which Mu is particularly proud of, and brags to everyone that they're the only family in Samoa with such a close connection to both kings).

A refrigerator where all the food was kept, and where all the ice-water bottles of Malaefou were kept, too. They didn't have a sefe, like us. That was too primitive (her mother's words).

A gas stove, too. Mu's family had a gas stove. The kind you just turned the button and fire came out.

I remember the first time we saw that. We were amazed and amazed. It was the most fascinating thing. It was the topic of our conversations for days—weeks. Until Elisa returned from New Zealand with her hair dyed blond.

A pick-up truck.

A taxi.

The *only* store in Malaefou, Vaiala and Malaetuai where everyone had a black book...and Mu kept teasing us about not paying the book off on time. She said that her mother said they should call them Kusi Aiafu instead of Aikalafu...which we closed our ears to.

A plantation, too. Yes, a plantation. On Saturdays or on holidays her family hired the Aufaipese to weed their plantation. It was *that* big. Too big for a family of fifty-four members to keep, even though they had two lawn mowers and weedkiller.

Yes, we were envious of Mu and tried desperately by association to be her friend. If not that, then just to be seen with her, to sleep over at her house—since they had the best evening meals which were served every night and their house was always joyous because of this. They sang evening hymns in loud angelic voices because their stomachs always knew they were going to be filled...unlike most of us whose voices improved only with pay-day, which was every fortnight.

Yes, we wanted to be seen with Mu, even though she was a faikakala and a mikamika vale, bragging and bragging. Up and down. Down and out. Brag-brag-brag some more about how rich they were and how no one could touch her because she had such a big 'aiga.

'But, you're dumb!' I yelled out...and Moa too, in her very

beer-bottle voice which only I could hear.

'You're as dumb as a...' Moa's voice taking on visible form now. 'So dumb I can't even compare you to an animal or an object. You're only at Samoa High School because Eleele is friends with the principal...and you cheated on your exams...and, and, and...'

'So what?' Mu snapped back at Moa—which meant us all. 'So what? You're just jealous...jealous that your own parents don't know anyone and that you have to go to Vaimauga, and none of you have relatives in Australia or Amelika.'

Silence. Complete silence. The kind you hear before you tell a lie, or when someone's creeping into the sefe in the middle of the day or night, or when a baby is asleep, or when a spider weaves a web. Silence. Some of the girls who didn't have relatives in any of the foreign lands mentioned above stood up slowly and moved out of the relative counting circle without saying a word, without even wishing us good night.

The more stubborn ones—like Ela, Salala, Moe, Fale, Sieni, Talalelei, Moa, and me—stayed behind to defend the little dignity left to us...to justify with extravagant vocabulary, which we knew Mu did not know, anything that needed justification.

Try as we might to contradict her, we knew deep down that she was right. Those simple words she used—'But you have no relatives in Australia! Or Amelika!'—stabbed us in the back, in the front, everywhere.

She was always right when it came to relatives. And we always knew that when it came to this, we hated relative counting—hated-hated-hated it—and blamed boring nights for allowing it to happen. We hated Mu, too (especially), not so much because she bragged-bragged-bragged, and kept bragging (Moa did that all the time about being the first 'aiga to have a paipa surrounded with tin, and one of the few 'aiga with indoor plumbing, and most importantly for being the second youngest in Malaefou to be acknowledged by the moon). We hated Mu because she spoke the dreadful truth, making us realize how poor we really were. Most of our own relatives lived in Malaefou still, or in kua back villages, or worst even, in Savai'i. I, for example, only had five 'aiga in far-away countries...in a far away country, that is New Zealand. None in Australia. None in Amelika...as Mu loved to point out.

Sasa, my mother's oldest brother, was married to a Maori who sewed shoes and dresses while Sasa was laid-off...again. He sat at home all day watching TV, eating-drinking, or going off to the tracks to spend all that she earned...which he called 'our money.' Thank God they had no children. This according to old man Misiluki who visited them once for Christmas and returned home with no oso...not even lollies.

Another 'aiga who didn't contribute to anything—but we counted her still because she is in New Zealand—was Lupesa, my father's youngest sister who was on a government scholarship. She was in school still and couldn't earn any money.

'Yet,' she would say.

Each time she wrote, the card was empty.

Fue was my father's oldest sister, who married old (at twenty-eight) and took seven years to conceive a child. She had her insides tied after the second child.

'Or else she'd have died,' said the palagi doctor.

She is married to a palagi, who tried hard to ignore our existence or that Lupe had a Samoan family.

'Too much faalavelave,' he said, and refused to have his kids speak Samoan…which Fue perpetuated, naming her children Charlene and Christopher. She sent money only twice a year: for Tausi's birthday and for Christmas.

'She has no alofa,' said everyone here. 'She's been poisoned by the palagi.'

His name we don't care to know, but called him only le pua'a elo, rotten pig.

Poasa, my cousin, was a pastor in a place called Papato'eto'e. He was the only one with real Samoan children, a real Samoan wife, a real Samoan heart. Everyone here said as much. Poasa converted to the Mormon church in Papato'eto'e, which disturbed everyone a bit still. But, he was accepted. Every time he wrote he enclosed pamphlets of happy papalagi blowing horns…which were thrown immediately into the evening fire. The money was kept and given as incentives to Samuelu, our pastor.

'Poasa has a good heart,' said everyone, 'no matter whose horn he blows.'

The last of my relatives was perhaps the most embarrassing in the history of New Zealand…and of Malaefou, especially. Iopu—named after the good prophet and most favourite son of the Filiga family—was sent to New Zealand to become an accountant, but found his way instead into a prison in Aukilagi, put there because he 'accidentally dropped' a full beer bottle onto the face of a bus driver who told him that beers were not allowed on the bus. The bus driver's head was cut wide open and air escaped into it. He nearly died…this according to Moa's cousin Filisi, who was drunk together with Iopu during that most unfortunate of incidents. His name was thrown at our faces as an example of true failure whenever someone got pissed or cross with any of our 'aiga.

Filisi was the only relative Moa had in New Zealand. He fixed cars and trucks and buses, and was married to a Rarotongan.

'That's where all his sweat goes!' said the women of Moa's 'aiga. 'That woman will eat and eat and eat all that he has, until he goes to the grave.'

Moa's five brothers—Manu, Esau, Filemu, Lomitusi and Junior—migrated to American Samoa, working-work at the fish factory. They bought a house in Utulei and took in guests from here who went there looking for jobs or wives to make them citizens...or just visiting.

Now Mu's relatives, 'aiga and relatives...

'Who wants to count my relatives?' she mocked us, and mocked us, daring-daring us. She picked me...not because she liked me or anything, but because she pitied me.

'Why don't you do it, Alofa? You know them all, anyway.'

And I did. She was right, I did.

Bitter as it was, I was the one who loved counting her 'aiga— I loved it and hated it, but loved it more. Because for a while there I could pretend, pretend through my knowledge that they were my uncles, my aunties, my cousins...my 'aiga. So I took up the challenge, clearing my throat first, coughing out all the mucus stuck there...and I began with Pola and Lalolagi, Mu's grandparents.

Pola and Lalolagi lived in Malaefou, and had been to New Zealand, Amelika, Australia more times than someone running to and fro from a serious diarrhoea attack. Pola and Lalolagi had two daughters and fourteen sons. Aoao and Fiasili lived in Amelika, and had between the two of them eight children who all went to school, went to work and understood Samoan (but didn't speak it).

Efu the middle-middle (named after Pola's brother who went fishing one day and never returned), Faaali, Sausaunoa, Fa'imoto, Laulau, Tausua, Samasoni (who is not strong at all) lived in Australia and had between them all and their palagi wives twenty afa-kasi children and five grandchildren. 'Aiga Lalolagi of Malaefou district was heard constantly on the radio at nights to collect express mail from the post office twice or six times a month.

Laulelei, Pola's favourite son, because he was sick from asthma and couldn't breathe correctly...Laulelei, who was named after Lalolagi's father who had only one leg (the other was too sweet of sugar and had to be cut off, said the doctor...something we girls never understood)...Laulelei lived in New Zealand with his Tongan wife, Mili, whose womb was dead. But everyone loved her still, because she shipped home clothes and food.

'There's a good woman for ya!' said everyone. 'There's a good woman.'

Misiafa and Tomasi lived in Tokelau and Fiji respectively. Misiafa was a pastor in Tokelau and lived there with his Samoan wife, Fiapito, and five children who all spoke Tokelauan. They didn't send money, but dried fish and a Tokelau Bible which was actually a Samoan bible. And they visited always every Christmas.

'Why do they even bother coming if that's all they bring?' the women mumbled and mumbled.

And Tomasi, named after the good apostle and converted to the Pope's church, was studying to be a brother in Fiji and lived with people called San Franciscans.

Lautolo and Launiu—twins who were dwarfs and the best

cricket players in Malaefou—lived in Malaefou. Lautolo worked at the Department of Agriculture and came home with food confiscated from tourists or visitors from American Samoa. While Launiu drove the family taxi, picking lots of girls up especially and driving them around for free, just so that he could be seen with them…which made everyone laugh.

Eleele and Elisa, Mu's mother and her sister. Elisa was sent to New Zealand to take care of her brother, Laulelei, while Mili worked at the shoe factory. Elisa never got married. She remained pure, until her first check-up at the hospital when a metal instrument injured her hymen. Everyone laughed about this embarrassing story. All these years and she was saving it for a piece of metal. Ha!

And Mu's mother, Eleele, the most ruthless woman in Malaefou, who beat her sons' wives up, and ran their store, and drove their pick-up, and was afraid of cockroaches and dust. She married Mu's father, the son of the Minister of Finance. He was never allowed to come down from the pedestal he was put on.

Yes, they were all alive…every single one of them. So blessed with God's wealth were Pola and Lalolagi.

'So blessed they are,' said everyone in Malaefou.

And I wove on and on the story of my 'aiga—Mu's 'aiga that was—until the moon fell between mountains and rivers, and flying foxes were asleep, too.

Someone called out our names, 'O mai i kokogu! Makuai kaukalaiki kele!'

'The night is old,' they yelled out, 'and you have no business sitting out there, in the wind, in the moon, in the wind, in the dark…'

TAUSI'S RULES

- Girls should never dry themselves with the same towel a boy or a man has used.
- Girls should try and avoid wearing each other's panties and bras.
- Girls should always volunteer to do housework.
- Girls should avoid eavesdropping at all times.
- Dress yourself good when you're going to Apia.

Lesi asked, 'Can I come with you?'

'For the last time, no!'

I pulled on my only pair of jeans, which everyone in the village knew I wore to Apia every Saturday. But, I did not care. Most of them didn't have a pair of their own. I did the ritual of pulling the 'Jesus loves me' T-shirt over my head... brightly yellow.

'Can I come with you?'

I combed my hair, rubbing Sione's hair-grease into my curls. Comb-comb...comb straight...making the hair go straight... making the hair look like Jill's hair on *Charlie's Angels*. I knew what they would say.

'O le fia Jill ia o lea mea ailalafa! Kope le seluga o ou fugu koeikiiki sau le pasi! Akoa le kausaga o ku koeikiiki ka'e le kioaka i le…'

I closed my ears…closed my hair to their mumble-mumble. Mumblings—they were just jealous because they were too old and they couldn't fit into anything.

'Faapaku i luga lou ulu! Can I come with you?'

I pulled the hair together in a bun, and held the bun with the back of a turtle formed into a comb…a buncomb. Then over to Pisa, who gave me the twenty tala.

'*Please*, can I come with you?'

Pisa gave me the verbal list.

'Kasi le kaukalo, coconuts, taro leaves, esi a le loomakua aua gei galo, a pumpkin…'

'Pisa, can I go with Alofa?'

'…curry, three pounds of sugar, a basket of breadfruit, and a bag of turkey asses.'

'This is not enough,' I protested.

'That's enough,' the voices said. 'She's keeping the change and buying cigarettes with it. Did you know that she already smokes?'

'Pepelo ia (they're lying),' I said.

Lesi: 'Lokoleaga ia ia, Alofa!'

'She's going to the movies for sure before she goes to the market. That's why she doesn't wanna take Lesi with her!'

'Pepelo ia,' I said

(They're lying shits. Eat shit eat…shit and choke while you're doing it, you, you…)

'She's wearing makeup, Lupe,' said the voices. 'I think you

should beat her up before she goes, before she…'

Sugar Shirley: 'Leave her alone, kou faipopolo! Get your butts off to the sea and do something useful, like try and catch a kuikui. There's a challenge for you! Catch it before it runs off with a seaweed or a fugafuga.'

'Ha! Malo Sugar Shirley.'

'Don't laugh, Alofa. Here's the rest of the money. You better not use it on anything else but on the things that I told you to—do you understand?'

'Yes.'

'You better, because Peka is selling today. I better not hear anything with your name in it this evening. You do want to go to Malua next week, don't you? Take Lesi and Sale with you.'

Sale: 'Do I have to go? I was supposed to meet Iopu today for the galuega. We're helping the faifeau build a fence around Lele's grave.'

Pisa: 'Are you gonna eat there tonight and tomorrow? Then tell Iopu to tell Moe or Pale or Filiga or Iosua or Vai or Masaga or, or, or…to help build the fence. You have to go with your sister to the market to get food to feed the living, do you understand?'

'But…'

———

I hopped onto the bus with Lesi and Sale. Lesi was all ready for Apia since she finished eating breakfast…since she finished collecting the leaves and cigarette buds off the paepae. She had been bragging all morning to Oli and Saulelei.

'I'm going to Apia! I'm going to Apia! Alofa is taking me to Apia!'

38

Sale wore a sharkface.

'You better not say anything to me, Alofa. Do you understand?'

'I don't even want you to come with us. You can get off at the next stop. I won't say anything. I'll find someone at the market to help carry everything. Go!'

He disappeared, and I was left holding Lesi on my lap because the bus was full. Full of cologne, and oils, and pigs, and feet, and Palmolive soap, and babies...all the way to Apia. All the way to Apia I carried in my hair (which I let down when I entered the bus) Pisa's list for the Sunday umu and Fa'afetai's favour ('Buy me some lopa and Marlboros, if you can').

One of the men, Vainuu, who got off the bus from Mulifanua was a mourner and was accompanied by two dead pigs wearing hibiscus around their ears and noses. The man was a faipele who was a faithful Christian and a faithful Samoan. He spoke with animals. He spoke with the wind. He spoke with water, even. This was his first trip to Apia. The two pigs were attracting flies and the flies decided to marry the pigs—despite the man's curses.

'These pigs are already married,' swore Vainuu. 'They're married to a dead cousin who is waiting for them. Get out of here.'

The Apia flies were surprised that a human spoke their language and out of excitement stuck to the pigs.

'You are le migao,' said Vainuu to the flies. 'You will die before we reach Malaefou.'

Vainuu asked a young man who was standing next to the public toilet, 'Where is the pulu of Malaefou?'

The young man pointed to the direction of the wharf. Vainuu gathered the two pigs and started walking in that direction. The young man called out, 'There's a bus that goes there. It's much farther than it looks.'

But Vainuu was nowhere to be seen.

LE AU GIUSILA

Our 'aiga was the first in Malaefou to get a TV, even if it was black and white, and most kids said it didn't count and that Mu's 'aiga was actually the first since they had it coloured and clearer, and much, much larger than ours.

We got the TV from New Zealand via my grandmother's brother's son, Misipati, who bought it from an American family who lived there in New Zealand. Our relatives there thought it better to send the TV to us in Samoa...in Malaefou.

That week, before the TV arrived, everyone wanted to be our friends.

Fiafia and Faanoanoa—twins who were six months older than me, and who never spoke to me directly, but teased me about bringing leftovers to school and wearing panties with the Dunlop tyre rubber waist and that I peed in bed until I was nine—suddenly gave wide smiles whenever we met. The kind of smiles you see at stores on Santa Claus at Christmas, or on a girl with yellow hair and white teeth on the side of a box of toothpaste. They would offer pencils at pastor's school whenever the eye of my pencil died. They would offer a sharpener to resurrect the eye of the pencil. They would offer to comb and fili my hair in a style they knew I did not know. They would say 'ku-lou' whenever they passed me—even though they were older. And told me their deep, deep secrets—that they stole cigarettes from Leaga, their father, who never suspected them and that their father would beat Epenesa their brother up for it; that they cheated on the Sunday School Final; that they saw Donna the fa'afafige 'do it' to Leauvaa, who is supposed to be sick for girls only.

In addition, they invited me once to sleep over at their house and offered me the cleanest and prettiest sheets, the biggest pillow with a 'Jesus is the Reason' pillowcase. And I was allowed to use the Palmolive soap first before they washed their hair. This was a luxury, for my family washed only with Fasimoli Ka Mea, laundry soap.

Their mother asked me that night, if I could ask Pisa to send someone over when *Fantasy Island* came on. I told her that I would, and that I would run over personally, and that she should stay also for *Days of Our Lives*.

'They're unmasking Roman tonight!'

She said she would stay on and that I was a good girl, a fine influence on her daughters. But she also said that I should try to stay away from that Lili.

'She's too old to hang around you girls, isn't she? You can sleep over whenever you want...whenever your father allows.'

—

Everyone was too excited the night the TV arrived. We all knew its history before we even saw it: that it was an American TV bought from an American couple by Misipaki and that it was arriving here to make Malaefou history. Before the TV arrived, kids were already choosing what they wanted to see:

Charlie's Angels;
The Bionic Woman;
Star Trek;
Big Time Wrestling.

The elders were already saying that everyone in school should go to bed when the *Love Boat* came, which was fine with all of us. Who wanted to see a bald-headed captain steering a ship full of morons around anyway?

That night, after the evening meal (which was early and quick), everyone rushed to the front of the house. Kids were fighting and pulling hair—and pulling more hair—over who would get to be closer to the TV.

'You should all move back,' said Asu, my father's brother, who thinks he owns everything in the house…even though he's unemployed, and never went to school, and has no kids of his own (who would want to marry him?), and is big, and has a big voice, and rules us like a dog rules cats.

'Not too close or you'll go blind! No one is to touch the TV, understand? No one. Any of you kids caught touching the TV is going to be wrapped up in their sheets and thrown out into the paepae. Do you understand?'

We nodded our heads, too excited to listen. We just wanted to see moving pictures.

After Asu finished explaining the TV rules, he plugged the TV in and switched it on. Nothing came out. He took the plug out and tried it again, but still nothing happened.

'Where are the pictures?' we all asked. 'Where are the pictures?'

Faleniu our neighbour, who works for the Public Works in Apia, came over to the TV and spoke to Asu.

'That the TV won't work without an antennae or a transformer.'

'What are those?'

While Faleniu explained to Asu and to all the older boys and men of the fale who were gathering now around the TV what a transformer was and why American stuff would not work here in Malaefou, the women of the house (half-disappointed, half-embarrassed) were heard shouting.

'Damn those New Zealanders!'

'Damn that Misipaki!'

'Who does he think we are?'

'Bake him in an oven!'

'Bake them all in an oven!'

'Damn! damn! damn!'

The village children cried.

'Your TV is broken!'

'Your relatives in New Zealand are not rich enough to send a TV that works!'

—

Three months later Filiga found an antennae and a transformer. Mr Brown was returning to his Australia, and wanted to sell his antennae and transformer for 250 tala. Filiga borrowed the money at work, which meant we had to take leftovers to school ...forever.

The actual antennae and transformer, sent by the relatives in New Zealand, was recovered later (much, much later) at Valu's house.

Valu was the Customs Inspector and had confiscated a refrigerator from American Samoa that he was using to make ice and other things.

'AIGA–FILIGA was marked in large bright red capital letters on the bottom of the transformer Valu had been using and using for months now.

Eseese the secretary noticed this and notified the men of our family, but only after Valu told her he loved his wife and was going back to her. The men of our family approached Valu with heavy fists and threats and all. In which case, Valu offered them a ham, two cans of pisupo, and an umbrella for the old lady.

'Never do this again! Understand? Never!'

This after many angry letters flew between New Zealand and Samoa.

The relatives in New Zealand wrote:

'You should have been happy! You were the first family to have a TV that came all the way from America to Misipati, who spent all his pay and sweat to buy it for you...and an antennae...and a transformer.'

The relatives in Malaefou were bitter at the relatives in New Zealand for sending something that didn't work and replied back:

'How do we know you sent a transformer...or an antennae? Why didn't you send them all together?'

'You're so ungrateful!' they wrote from New Zealand.

'You're so stingy!' the relatives here wrote back.

To prove they weren't stingy and that they had our best

interests at heart, the New Zealanders sent one hundred New Zealand dollars for the children's ipu, for Le Lotu A Tamaiti, which was used (more or less) to buy material, taro, kerosene, porridge for Tausi and the babies, Poker or Suipi.

Twenty tala was announced as the 'Aiga Filiga donation on White Sunday. A note was attached to the money.

> We are all well. We are sad that we could not be there to celebrate such a day with the whole family. We are thinking of you all and pray to God that we will see you again, soon.
>
> Sale's son, Iopu, is coming to Samoa for Le Loku A Kamaiki. He is bringing lollies for the kids, and shoes for Moe and Sita, and the old lady's white dress.
>
> *Alofaaga e tele mo outou,*
> Le Au Giusila.
>
> *p.s.* Please don't tell the old lady about the white dress. We thought it was better to be prepared. Who knows?

GIRL TESTS FOR TRUTH TELLING
OR HOW TO CATCH A LIAR

If you can jump rope with your eyes closed and cotton stuck in your ears and say the names of all your relatives at the same time, then you have passed the test for truth telling and it is clear that you don't wet mats at night.

If you can catch a sleeping butterfly between the thorns of a rose without spilling your own blood, then you have also passed the test and it is clear that you don't need to be accompanied to the toilet at night (when everyone is asleep and the path to the toilet is guarded by speaking owls and dirty old men).

If you can recite the twenty-three psalms backwards without taking a break, then you have passed the test that you don't dream.

If you can throw stones onto the sea and they bounce and bounce and bounce, then you have passed the test and it is clear that you can braid your own hair four ways.

If you can answer riddles and rhyme land animals with sea animals, then you have passed the test and it is clear that you don't like boys.

GHOST STORY

Ghost stories were what we especially loved listening to. I could never sleep for days after one of Vainuu's ghost stories. Vainuu was from Savai'i. He was my father's brother and a taulasea. He healed people who had the darkness sickness, or mai aiku as it is commonly known. Mai aiku is the sickness of ghosts. It is when an unhappy agaga reveals itself in the body of the living to show his unhappiness.

Whenever Vainuu visited Malaefou our house would be full of girls…and some boys, who were mostly fa'afafige.

'Do you get sad when Faanoanoa is sad? Do you get happy when Fiafia is happy? Do you feel pain when Faanoanoa feels pain? Did you know that twins die together?' asked Vainuu, addressing the village twins Fiafia and Faanoanoa. 'Well, they do …some.'

Vainuu told us once about twins in Savai'i.

'They were very beautiful. They were also identical, like you. It is said that one evening one of the twins was sitting outside the paepae on a rock, combing her hair. Her hair came down to her knees and it took a long time for her to get the knots out. She sat there and combed and combed and combed...and night fell and kept falling, and the girl kept combing. An aitu was looking at her, observing her every move. It is said that the aitu was in love with the twins and wanted to take them to Pulotu.

'The girl finished combing her hair and was about to start braiding it, when a beautiful bird appeared out of nowhere. The bird was blue and red and green, and it started talking to the twin.

'"I am going to take you with me.... I am going to take you with me.... I am going to take you with me...."

'The girl screamed but had no voice. She tried standing up, but the rock held her feet tight. Later on in the night someone found her body and carried her immediately into the fale. They covered her with blankets and women sang songs, and a faipele was brought to the house. The faipele laid down her cards, shook her head from side to side and left. The women of the house grinded vaisina in a rock and rubbed the girl's body from toe to head with it. Someone asked to take the girl to the hospital in Tuasivi, but one of the old women stopped them.

'"No," she said, "This is not a papalagi sickness; this is a Samoan sickness."

'The twin girl was crying and crying, and sang like a bird. Everyone was afraid of her—even her twin sister who was not affected by the sickness. Before the sun was born the next day, the bird-girl stopped singing and started talking in the voice of a man.

'"Don't be so self-centered. Don't be so vain, Laulii."

'Laulii was the girls' father. He was a matai, a faipule. He went to church every Sunday and every Wednesday, and never missed anything for Jesus Christ. He was a good man, everyone thought.

'"Don't be so self-centered. Don't be so vain."

'After the bird-girl said this she laughed a strange laugh—a loud strange laugh like the laugh of a drunken man. She smiled at everyone before she closed her eyes...and then she was dead.

'Two weeks later her sister, who by then was never left out of sight, was sitting on the same rock in the evening. She let down her beautiful hair and started combing and combing, when a beautiful flying-fish flew over her feet and told her, "I'm here to get you...I'm here to get you...I'm here to get you..."

'"But, you've already taken my sister," said the girl boldly. "What do you want with me?"

'Upon hearing this, the fish cried and cried and cried...and sang a song, confessing her love for the girl. And in the song she said, "I am your sister. I miss you so."

'When she heard this the girl embraced the fish and wiped the fish's tears with her long hair.

'"Take me with you.... Take me with you," she said.

'And the fish did. The fish took the girl by the hair, between his teeth, and flew into the sea...and her body was never found again. Whenever a strange bird is seen or whenever a flying fish is seen, children are warned to run into their fale, and close their eyes and face the ground. Never look into the eyes of a strange bird or a flying fish. Never talk to a strange bird or to a flying fish.'

FA'AFETAI—SUGAR SHIRLEY

Death struck our family when I was thirteen years old and my cousin Fa'afetai (Shirley Girl, Sugar Shirley) died accidentally.

Yet, it was not an accident.

'It is the will of God,' the old women in the village chanted.

The lamenting went on for weeks, starting on the night they found his body and on to the day they brought him home from Motootua. He was in a black dress Sisifo sewed and there were coins in his eyes, and Lina wanted to jump into the grave but the men stopped her right before she did.

All of Malaefou understood.

Old and young people wept only…only.

The whole village was wrapped in sadness.

—

Everyone had their own stories to tell about Shirley:

How she sat under the pulu combing her long hair.

How no one was allowed to touch that comb.

How she danced on fiafia nights, collecting the most money

51

from the audience.

How she knew all the songs, Samoan and palagi, ever played on the 2AP.

How she made the best curry the family and village had ever eaten.

How she teased old women, old men…anyone old.

(She was the only one allowed to do so. She was the only one who made them all laugh–laugh–laugh with some of the wildest jokes ever.)

—

Shirley was the only older boy in our family who talked to us girls, who laughed with us. She didn't yell at us like the others. She didn't order us around (like we ordered the younger ones:

'Go get my towel!'

'Go pick up the breadfruit leaves!'

'Go buy lollies at Fa'ameleas!'

'Go buy bread!'

'Go jump in the ocean…and drown yourself.'

…if they didn't listen.)

Shirley was a fa'afafige and s/he liked to dress like a girl. She had constant fights with the women of the house because she would parade around Apia in some of their best clothes, wearing their lipstick, blue eyeshadows, high-heel shoes, perfume…anything female.

'Oh, I'm not feeling well today,' she would tell seriously-devoted-to-God old women who cracked a smile only when she was around. 'It's that time of the month.'

'Don't do what I would,' she would say to us girls whenever

we left the house for the aufaipese at nights.

'I think I'm pregnant, but I don't know who the real father is,' she would embarrass boys of the Youth for Christ.

She never used the men's toilet and always sat down on the toilet seat.

No one dared called her a him. She was rarely called Fa'afetai —only by the faifeau and the old people of Malaefou. She was Shirley, and everyone called her Shirley, or Shirley Girl, or Sugar Shirley. No one dared call her a him. No one. But someone did… once.

—

She was a woman from Vaivase who had just married Falefou. Falefou is known as the best rugby player from Malaefou. He is also known for his uncontrolled temper. He had suddenly married Eleele dirt because, according to some women, he left a bread baking in her oven. She had the biggest mouth, too, pretending not to speak Samoan after she returned from a thirty-day stay in New Zealand.

It was cricket day. Cricket is the one game we all looked forward to…old men, old women, young men, young women, children, dogs, grasshoppers, everyone. Everyone loves cricket because it is the one game in which the whole village participates.

That morning we were sitting on the malae, collecting the money from each team, when Eleele marched over and asked me, 'O fea lei kama Shirley Boy?'

'It's Shirley Girl. How come you can't speak properly?'

Eleele (ignoring my warning and my question): 'Where's Shirley Boy?

I want to be on Shirley Boy's team.'

'She's massaging Tausi's back.'

Eleele: 'One of you girls write him down on my team.'

Moa: 'I wouldn't say that out loud if I were you.'

Eleele: 'Why not? Is he going to beat me up? Is he going to beat up a wo…man?'

Before Eleele could finish her thought, she was on the ground. Boom! Boom!

Sugar Shirley hovered over her timber-body.

'O le a le mea e ke faia ai ou kala, a?'

Yelling some more in her very feminine voice, 'Get up! Get up, you big mouth bitch!'

Eleele, like an emergency car siren, started screaming and screaming

'Auoi ka fia ola! Auoi ka fia ola!'

No one helped her. Everyone was either counting their money, or checking their bats, or doing something to avoid hearing or responding to Eleele's cry for her life, which was not in danger…'unfortunately,' some women mumbled.

Faleniu (smoking Samoan tobacco): 'She has to learn to control that mouth of hers.'

Ufi (rolling tobacco on a page from the *Samoa Weekly*): 'It's not like she didn't know.'

Laufai (opening the knot at the bottom of his lavalava, counting-counting): 'She provoked the boy.'

Fiasili (looking around and around, and then focusing on a bird in the sky): 'Better watch out for that husband of hers.'

Sieni (chasing the flies away from Pepe's nose): 'You mean Falefou? Do you think Tai gives a damn about Falefou?…or

Aoauli?…or Samasoni?…or about any of these so-called real men? Ha! You probably don't remember the day Tai beat the crap out of Samasoni and Iopu together, who were calling her a him. They say that was the busiest day Motootua had ever seen. They've never needed so much sewing-up in a day.'

Laughter…more laughter.

Ufi (passing the rolled tobacco to Faleniu who lights it): 'Well, he is a boy after all…a man, even. He should be able to control himself if he wants to be a woman. Ha!'

To everyone's surprise, Falefou ran over to the hysterical Eleele, punched her another one in the eyes and dragged her home.

Falefou: 'You're embarassing me in front of the village.'

Eleele: 'I'm leaving your goddamn village first thing tomorrow morning.'

Falefou: 'Why don't you leave now? Go pack the one dress you came with and get the hell out of here.'

Eleele: 'I'm taking Simi with me.'

Falefou: 'If you want to live to see your family, then you better go alone.'

———

The cricket game continued and Falefou was seen apologising to Sugar Shirley. Sugar Shirley was smiling, cracking jokes, and Falefou was heard laughing and laughing…

And someone was heard yelling out: 'Now that that woman is going back to her village, why don't you two tie the knot?'

And everyone laughed and laughed and laughed, until it was dark and people disappeared into their fale…leaving a blank sky behind.

The next day passed…and the next, and the next…and Eleele came over to our house with the head of a fish swimming in coconut milk, and taro, too, and bananas.

'For the old lady,' she whispered. 'For the old lady.'

—

It was palolo season and everyone was occupied in sewing ula mosooi and ula pua to attract the worms.

For us girls it was exciting because we met our stones, ma'a, boyfriends. No one would take notice. Everyone would be too busy scooping palolo into bowls or sacks. No one heard Fa'afetai's cries for help, when a wave hit him and pulled him towards the reef in the mist of that palolo excitement. His body, all purple, was found the next day on the beach, blown up twice its size. Crabs were already living in his mouth.

HAIRPINS AND HAIRPINS
AND WHAT BOYS LIKE BEST

Hairpins were dearer to us girls than they were to the boys. Boys used them to pick their ears. Girls used them in games, rarely in their hair.

The game of hairpins is called fa'aka pige and goes like this: it is played by two or more girls, depending on how large the circle is. A circle is drawn with a finger on the earth, or with a chalk on cement, or sometimes with a stick. One or two hairpins from each girl are placed in the centre of the circle. If the circle was drawn on the earth, a girl holds a little stone the size of a pigeon egg in her right or her left hand, and drops it onto the hairpin. If she is a good player, the hairpin should fly immediately out of the circle. Her opponent will be required to lay down another hairpin each time she is able to force a hairpin to fly out of the circle. A marble is used if the circle was drawn by chalk on cement.

This game is played and played during every recess in Apia—anywhere where there are cement, marbles, hairpins, or earth.

What fun!

Girls would jump up and down every time someone says 'let's play for hairpins!'

'How boring!' boys would say, every time they hear girls say 'let's play for hairpins!'

They'd rather be playing rugby or soccer, or marbles, too…or looking up some peacecorp's dress.

They do…di–do.

SHE WAS SIXTEEN WHEN THE EYE OF THE WATER BECAME CLEAR

She was sixteen when the eye of the water became clear and it was known throughout Malaelefou that Lili was pregnant. Her breasts were swollen. Her face looked so tired.

She had an appointment at Motootua.

Some said it was Iosua II. Others said she didn't know.

She was expelled from school.

This was all the whispering heard in every household before the eye of the water was finally cleared.

To this day, no one in Malaefou knows who the father was.

The baby was never carried to term. It came out a lizard. It came out a rat. It came out after the fourth moon.

I suppose no one really cared about the father of Lili's lizard because Lili was not the daughter of the faifeau or of a chief, or of someone with steady employment. She was a bad girl as far as the women of Malaefou were concerned, and it was rumoured even that she invited the lizard to her womb.

After the death of the lizard, Moa and I started talking to Lili.

'Did it hurt?' we asked her.

She only stared into the sky, nodding her head.

'I have the moon sickness,' said Moa.

This rather inappropriate confession, or rather Moa showing off, made me angry. She knew I did not have the moon sickness. She knew it, yet admitted to Lili with such casualness…as if boys even got it.

'Can you find me a cigarette?' Lili asked.

'We don't smoke—at least not in public,' I said in the lowest voice I could find.

'I'm not talking to you unless you find me a cigarette.'

—

An hour later we returned with a cigarette. It was a rolled Greys Moa stole from her grandmother's box. We knew, perhaps, that Lili was referring to an American cigarette when she said 'go get a cigarette.' We hoped our pretended ignorance was enough to convince her that we were worthy to talk to.

But, she wasn't there when we returned.

—

'Now what are we gonna do with this?'

'What if someone sees us returning it?'

'What if someone sees us holding it right now?'

'What if?'

We knew what the answers to our questions were. We would either get slapped on the mouth four times or more…beaten up if we were caught by an adult. Therefore, the most logical solution was to smoke it ourselves, thus ridding ourselves of the evidence completely.

We went to the beach at Falesasa. Falesasa was where the blind fool, Siniva, lived. We hid under the mosooi and lit the Greys. Moa took the first puff.

'This is how Lupe smokes,' she took the smoke into her lungs and returned it out her nose.

We laughed.

'That was good,' I said. 'Let me try it.'

'This is how Lafoga smokes.'

I took the smoke into my lungs and waited.

'You can do it,' said Moa.

'Poof! Cough! Cough!'

...and all the smoke came out of my mouth.

Moa laughed and laughed.

'That's what happens when you're imitating God's servant.'

We did this whenever we were alone and bored, imitating older people or dumb people or anyone peculiar. Moa continued laughing especially, because she was the only one who could accurately imitate Lafoga the faifeau smoking. Lafoga smoked like an umu...he literally did. You never saw smoke exit his mouth or nose.

'How does he do that, Moa?'

'Like this,' she said.

Moa took another drag and closed her eyes. I saw the smoke disappear into her. Her eyes were still closed when we heard the sudden sound of footsteps coming closer and closer. Moa dropped the Greys, stepped on it and covered it with leaves. I reached out to the mosooi that laid around and started stuffing them into my mouth, hoping-hoping that the mosooi would kill the scent of tobacco on my breath.

'So that's where you are!'

It was a female voice; it was a young voice. It was Lili! We both exhaled in relief. I spat the mosooi out of my mouth. It tasted like raw cashews.

'Don't scare us like that again.'

'Where's my cigarette, you little shits?'

—

We met again the next day, after Moa and I returned from school. It was a very good day. I remember it because it was the day we both found out that we passed the Form Two government examination, and that we were able to go on to High School. We were singing the latest Penina o le Tiafau hit when we heard the cry. We ran over to the side of the road to Misa's fale—an abandoned fale that was reserved for the rugby team and homebrew parties.

There she was, lying on the floor, her clothes all ripped apart, her face covered with blood. We couldn't believe what we saw. It was three in the afternoon.

'Who did this?'

'What happened?'

Lili was crying and crying and crying…and sobbing. Moa sat down and put Lili's head on her lap. I decided to go get help, but Lili said no.

'Don't, Alofa. I don't want anyone to know. You're not gonna say a word, okay?'

'Who was it?' I asked. 'I'm telling if you don't tell us who it was.'

'Shut up!' yelled Moa suddenly.

'You shut up,' I shot back.

'Shut your mouth and eat shit, and go get some water or do something. Can't you just grow up, Alofa?'

'It's alright, Moa,' said Lili. 'It's a fair exchange. It's my fault; I'm the one who wanted the secret in the first place. But you have to swear, you have to swear by your lives that no one else is to know about this.'

I had a strange feeling when Lili said those words. I felt like I already knew what she was about to say. I knew she was going to tell us something terrible, something ugly. I had the suspicion that whoever it was that did this to her planted the lizard in her womb. This thought terrified me. For a moment I sat there like a vaofefe, all curled up, all curled–curled up. One part of me wanted to know (to confirm?). The other, stronger part wanted ignorance…did not want to know.

Then the words came like a little hurricane, or perhaps a tornado…

'It was Iosua.'

…Picking my body up, swirling–swirling to the sky, past birds, past the coconut I've always wanted to climb…

'It was Iosua.'

…Silence. Body falling–falling to earth…

'It was Iosua.'

…Slapping against banyan roots…

'It was Iosua.'

…My whole skull breaking to pieces, and water spilling out…no blood, no blood.

After the revelation, or the confession, or however you might define it, Lili sat up from Moa's lap, put her head between her knees and squeezed. She sat in that position for a while, until the legs rose up suddenly and ran out of the fale; tripping and falling onto the paepae.

She reached out for a stone and started beating her head. I ran out to stop her, but Moa pulled me back by the hair.

'Don't,' she said. 'Don't.'

—

I didn't say a word for the rest of the day. I didn't even sing during the lotu that evening. What for?

'How can you allow this? Why didn't you stop it? If you know and see all, then you could have stopped Iosua from doing what he did. What kind of a god are you? I hate you. I hate you…and your equally hopeless son, Jesus Christ, too.'

This was the prayer I prayed before I drifted into sleep… before my body died a thousand deaths that night.

THE CENTRE

Apia, capital of the Independent State of Western Samoa. Apia, centre of all commercial and governmental activities, tourism, and trade. There is no consensus as to what the centre of Apia is. Everyone has their own version, their own definition, which varies in degree from one person to another.

—

Ask Fesili Aku-Iai, a Protestant-kiakogo-makai from Vaivase, sitting now in his faleo'o, playing solitaire with himself, fanning away the flies from the redness of the wound on his left toe...the wound caused when he tripped over the stack of Bibles and hymn books of the Aku-Iai family, stacked so nice and neatly there in the middle of the fale, on the sides of the fale, practically everywhere—Bibles practically everywhere.

He tripped while running after Piki the pig, who happened to cross the fale that bright Monday morning, licking all the New Zealand butter sitting on a tin plate on the mat there, too...in the middle of the fale, next to five loaves of hot bread from Falaoa's store, next to the stack of hymn books and Bibles.

A broken glass fell accidently from the book of Genesis, exodusing Fesili's body...ripping away at his flesh...travelling to the marrow.

Blood ran out...kept running and running, until Filemuepeiolelupeuatulelauolivemalueleononaonafaauoiaue, or Aue his wife, ran from the front house with a stick, lifted the bleeding foot above Fesili's beating heart and beat the blood—commanding it to go back to where it came from.

The blood obeyed immediately under the talking stick, sealing itself up into a wound the size of the Dental Care Unit at Motootua National Hospital...the wound staring now at his face, black with flies.

He waves at them—they fly away (a nine of spades on a ten). He waves again—they fly away (queen of hearts on a king). Waves...waves...whispering softly, too, to himself, as he lays another ten on a jack...on a queen...on a king.

Ask him, 'In your opinion, sir, what is the centre of Apia?'

And there would be no answer. No answer, indeed. Not a single word. Fesili will not utter one word. He will scratch his beard first...forming his index and middle fingers into a scissors...pressing them, ever so slightly, to his lips...making the questioner aware of the fact that he was once a smoker and that this is the universal sign for bumming a cigarette, or 'sharing one's worldly possessions,' as he would call it.

Sometimes the questioner will be a non-smoker and clueless to this sign, so universal in Fesili's mind.

'How can a fool miss it?'

Then he'll just walk away, leaving whoever it was that asked him feeling like they had just been talking to a horse, driftwood, or an operator up at the Post Office.

On the other hand, if you pick up on the little sign that is *so* universal to Fesili's mind, he will respond quite happily...after his third or tenth trip of fingers pressed to his lips. That's when you'll have him talking in his very cool manner, lower lip curled all the way to the upper lip, eyes closed, fingers rubbing his forehead (damp from fly piss), scratching his elbows now, adjusting his ie-solosolo. He'll look up and stare you straight in the nose, with one arm folded to the side of his ribcage while the other swings, or flys in the sky or in the hair of whoever it was that asked him about the centre.

Then his mouth opens ever so slightly, avoiding any unnecessary words or spit, practically whispering his very articulate, well thought-out description of the place he loves oh, so much.

He will begin by stating a fact—common among any good member of the LMS—and he will say it proudly, and loudly, too (especially if there was a pastor passing or any other member of the church he recognizes) that the centre of Apia is the Ioane Viliamu building. The Ioane Viliamu building because it's the highest building in Apia (and in Samoa), the strongest building in Apia (and in Samoa), and the holiest, too...next to all the Protestant churches dotted around the coast.

'The Ioane Viliamu building,' continues Fesili Aku-Iai—warming up now, pointing his fingers to the sky, to the sun, to the moon, to a missile in the sky—in a *most* interested tone (although not overly enthusiastic, but enthusiastic enough to keep whoever's listening listening), 'was built by the followers of the London Missionary Society in memory of John Williams, the missionary palagi (or 'breaker of the sky') who sailed to Sapapali'i in his Savali o le Filemu (or 'Messenger of Peace') in 1830, saving Malietoa Vainu'upo, his 'aiga, and the whole of Samoa from the terrible darkness they were living in.'

—

Soia Le-Guguku-Sole-Fesili-I-Ke'i-Ua-Lua-Fekoa'i-Ma-Se-Fagakikili, a Catholic woman from Moamoa, might just say the opposite: that the centre of Apia is the Cathedral...the Catholic Cathedral, that is.

Soia has been a widow for the last thirty years. She has thirteen living daughters—who have married and migrated to all the four corners of the world, some remaining in Samoa serving her every need—and two sons, twins, named after a palagi who interviewed them on sex, status, and domestic violence, and some other white woman who lived on Tau sixty or so odd years ago.

Freeman (Pagoka-ua-faasaolokoiga) and Derek (Keleki) both turned out to be fa'afafige. Keleki returned from Hawai'i with breast implants, and Pagoka-ua-faasaolokoiga leads a life of sin in Apia with sailors and unhappily or happily married men. Soia does not speak to them both. Not to Keleki especially...for mutilating God's image. She's given up praying for them, too, and doesn't mention them at all in her prayers...prayers that are full of praises to God, for keeping the whole family safe from the cars of Apia, keeping all the relatives in 'foreign lands' safe from cars, too, in general.

Soia Le-Guguku-Sole-Fesili-I-Ke'i-Ua-Lua-Fekoa'i-Ma-Se-Fagakikili is a healthy seventy-five-year-old woman who is served by all her children, grandchildren, and great-grandchildren, and is respected by the village of Moamoa for her age and her ability to still win the most cash on bingo nights.

She is the oldest woman in Moamoa and is considered by most to be the wisest. She weeds the grass around her husband's grave (every other day), polishing too, with wet rags the blueness and redness of the plastic flowers laid there as offering from her great-grandchildren in Australia to their dead great-grandfather, of whom they had heard a lot since growing up...and practically worshipped, in the form of the only existing photograph of him as a young teenager (sitting on the docks of the wharf in Malaefou, holding up a can of worms and three Steinlagers on a hook).

That poor boy could not catch a fish to save his own life.

Nevertheless, 'our great-grandfather was the best fisherman in the whole of Samoa,' they will brag to their friends in New Zealand, America, Lithuania, or wherever they happened to be... while Soia, their great-grandmother, sits in the coolness of the Moamoa breeze, fanning flies from her nose, sewing pillow cases, eating octopus tentacles, and thinking a lot about Jesus Christ—although not necessarily in that order.

Spiritually—or rather, religiously—Soia never misses morning mass, afternoon mass, and evening mass, confessing the same sins over and over again for the last thirty years with black beaded rosary slipping through her fat fingers.

She makes sins up just to have something interesting to say. Like, she spied on two dogs doing it last week, next to her husband's grave.

'Is this a sin, Father...or a sign for something?'

Is it a sin, too, to watch her eighty-year-old neighbour,

Solomona, take showers at night. Her sight is not the best. She's as blind as a bat, she swears. Is this, too, a sin? After all, it's been thirty years!

Fathers Francis Boaz and Faʻipula Beaglehole are aware of this but bless her anyway, giving her five Hail Marys and a cultural controversy each time she draws the curtain and leaves the confession box...the scent of coconut hanging always in the air she leaves behind.

Yes, Soia doesn't care about Apia...doesn't care about the nature/nurture thing, either. But, most of all she really doesn't care about Apia...doesn't care about all the sin that goes on there. She lives in Moamoa, and if it weren't for that Cathedral i Mulivai she would swear that Moamoa is the centre of Apia...of Samoa, even. But for Jesus's sake, and more importantly for the sake of her own soul, she will identify that Cathedral as the centre where one fourth of the Apia population worship in flowery dresses, golden crosses and high-heel shoes...English mass once every Sunday and Samoan mass twice, sometimes ten times a day.

—

On the more vernacular side of things Alaisa Fiaola-Confusion, the half Chinese boy from Alamagoto, might think of the kung-fu theater in Taufusi as the centre of Apia.

The kung-fu theater is also the Fale Kifaga o Saiga or 'House of Movies of the Chinese.' It is surrounded by Chinese restaurants, shops, restaurants, more shops...and Bruce Lee posters plastered all over.

Alaisa Fiaola-Confusion hangs out under the posters of Bruce Lee with his friends, drinking coca-cola (if they have money), chewing the salt out of dried chinese plums or lole saiga, as they are commonly known.

Alaisa is known among his friends as a cry-baby and a liar. He cries whenever someone is not listening to one of his stories, which are usually about the movies they have all just seen, or about adults or bats or cats having sex.

He is teased repeatedly by girls for being a pervert—one who spies on his own parents, for Christ's sake. And he is also teased by boys, his own friends, for having rice eyes and a small penis.

Alaisa hates this so, telling them all to go to hell…and that his eyes are perfectly fine…and that he can see with them…and that his penis will grow when he grows—just wait and see!…and that he's never seen his parents do 'it' he swears.

—

Tu Lou, the cricket ball maker from Kapakapao, thinks (economically) without questioning of Le Fale o Pakele or Bartley's as the centre of Apia. Centre—because that's where she and her eight-month-old baby, Si-mea, sit and sit, eating lopa, crackling gum, selling-selling her handmade cricket balls, fans, and coconut ear-rings…if she made some that week.

Tu is twenty-seven years old, has kinky hair, short build, small feet—small-small feet—and a smile that betrays to anyone her being a descendant of a Solomon Island indentured labourer, brought over to Samoa by the Germans to work in their coconut plantations, cocoa plantations and to build roads, which nowadays all the cars of Apia appreciate.

Tu's grandmother was from Vaiala, a taupou who was prac-tically disowned when the family found out she had lost her virginity…and to a meauli of all things. The family, greatly shamed, wiped Tu's grandmother (whose name is still unknown because no one will talk about her) completely out of their memories…vowing never to remember her, killing her off, even when she was still living. She was banished to Kapakapao where no one lived at that time, where no one at Vaiala could possibly see her and say, 'Le keige Vaiala lale ga pau i le meauli.'

Or worse even, 'That's one of Esimoko's girls who married that maguki.'

It wasn't really until twenty years later that anyone from the Esimoko family caught up on Tu's grandmother's existence…or rather, her non-existence. She had died from the great influenza of 1918, leaving behind seven healthy sons and three daughters who followed her to the grave. Now Tu Lou, her granddaughter, sits at Le Fale o Pakele—the place she calls the centre—weaving a fan, crackling gum, waiting (patiently) for cricket fans to come to Apia.

—

Alu E-Su'e-Gi-Fafie-O-Le-Saka, the elevator man, thinks however of the clock—the Fale o Pipi—and the NPF building as the centre of Apia. He thinks this because he works at the NPF building. All day long he sits on a grey stool, pushing the numbers 1–2–3–4–5–6, telling off snotty school brats who tease him for pushing the wrong buttons.

'Take the stairs!' he would yell back at them.

Or, 'I know your father! I'll tell Makauli on you!'

Alu wipes the sweat off the top of his lips after the brats flee.

'Bloody wankers!' he mumbles. He is the elevator man. He

helps everything go up and down.

—

Up and down too is Roseline Vain or Losa Fiaaulelei, the nineteen-year-old afakasi girl from Lelata whose family won the national lottery last week...and everyone thought it was a hoax. How come a Samoan never wins these things? Wearing mufty now in the middle of the day. Sitting in her family's brand new van, going up and down, up and down...and wearing red lipstick, too.

And English, too. Spitting English, too. Too-ti-too between the gaps in her teeth, with the car parked there on the corner of the Nelson Public Library and the RSA...which she thinks is the centre of Apia.

The 'centre' because that's where she waits for 'him,' pretending to read a book while she waits for him. Him, the son of Alu the elevator man, who she's been after for the past year. Considered by all females the most handsome beau in the whole of Apia. Chosen by the Rugby Union to represent Samoa in the First Fifteen playing in Hong Kong next month.

—

The dead dogs of Apia don't give a damn about the centre. Nor do the pigs, guava and mango leaves. They don't waste time thinking about where things are. Nor do they care to name them. They just *know*. So they live and die knowing them, singing-and-talking knowing them, laughing knowing them, shitting-and-pissing knowing them, knowing that despite what people say the Makeki Fou i Savalalo or New Market is the centre...always has been, always will be.

From the eye of a fish the sea at the Makeki Fou smells of dead dogs, mango leaves, and elegi tin-cans. Waves cry diesel tears and banana peels, oil, and human shit, too. The sun hangs there like a pumpkin with a ten tala sign written in ink taped around it's belly. Pumpkins think they taste like Palmolive soap under the sun and eels swim, too—in coconut oil or alone in their own oil, soaked there in banana leaves since six o'clock. Buses arrive thirsty every ten minutes from Motootua National Hospital, Malaefou, Aleipaka, Mulifanua, Afega, Falefa, and many other points of origin. They bring with them men and women, pigs and fish, chicken and Christmas carols, taro and bananas, taamu and tauaga, iekoga and babies, old lavalavas...and Jesus Christ, too—breaking Last Supper bread in purple velvet, guarding the newest music from American Samoa.

The men and women, and pigs and fish, and chicken, and taro, and bananas, and taamu and tauaga, and Christmas carols, and iekoga and babies, and old lavalavas exit the bus after they each deposit twenty sene, or one tala, or five tala fifty sene, or seven tala—depending on age and the distance travelled—in the little box in front of the bus driver, who collects them all and smiles at the passengers...and tells them to 'have a good time in Apia.'

It costs four tala for a live pig from Mulifanua to visit Apia. It costs half that for a dead pig. Babies are free...babies ride for free, too. Free, too, is that big Apia pumpkin, strung up between clouds...shining-shining through the clouds.

Trees dance to the carols of Christmas, floating under the hot August pumpkin.

And a policeman's lavalava is blown up to his face by the obnoxious wind, who knows that the policeman never wears underwear and that, instead of tattoos, he has lafa spread all across his behind.

—

A newspaper boy makes the rounds, 'Faakau gusipepa! *Samoa Weekly!* The continuing story of Taki ma Lisa! Faakau gusi!'

His voice fades into the steam, rising from the tar, rising from the moa of Samoa—the mid, the centre.

—

Samoa was once sacred to Moa. Moa was the son of Rocks. Rocks married the Earth and the Earth was pregnant and a male-child was born and he was called Moa. His father Salevao, god of the rocks, called his son after the moa (the middle, the centre, the motion in the middle of his mother's womb).

Salevao ordered that the umbilicus be laid on a club and cut with a sharp stone. Thus all objects were sa ia Moa, sacred to Moa.

Vai (water) was sent down from the heavens to wash Moa and it, too, was sa ia Moa, sacred to Moa.

Moa's mother, Laueleele, wanted more water to drink. Laueleele was thirsty from giving birth. Thus water was sent from the heavens via the stomachs of bamboo. Pools and springs and rivers were thus born.

Salevao wanted to be lost in stones. He wanted to loose his mana in ma'a...in the soil. Everything that grew out of the soil would be sa ia Moa, sacred to Moa—taro, bananas, taamu, mangoes. Maggots were sa ia Moa. So were the rocks and the earth. Everything was sacred. Until Moa became a man and grew hair... hair longer than a fautasi, darker than lama.

Moa's hair was cut and returned to the heavens. This was the only way for the sa to be lifted. And even after it was the sacredness of everything was known still as sa ia moa. So is the name 'Samoa.' So is Samoa. Selling newspapers in the steam of tar. Driving buses under pregnant clouds. Directing buses under pregnant clouds, under a cheeky wind.

—

Noon. Burners are busy-busy. Pans and pots, spoons and forks, teeth and knives, napkins and fingers, fingers and fingers are busy-busy too. Scooping rice, counting pennies, stirring mutton flaps, biting turkey asses, licking pork lard and lipstick, too… some lips do. While other mouths chew and chew and chew: sugar cane/fasipovi masima/german buns/tobacco. Old women smoke Samoan tobacco wrapped in the business section of the *Samoa Times,* the *Observer,* and other non-decipherable hieroglyphics. Other times, tobacco is wrapped in the written-in-Samoan *Samoa Weekly* or the *Sun's* 'Continuing Drama of the Week.' But only after the continuing drama of that week has been read, re-read, and discussed over and over with pumpkin customers, vendors, and the occasional peacecorps worker who speaks near-perfect Samoan…near-perfect because he speaks only the *t* and not the *k.*

Rarely is tobacco wrapped in banana leaves…rarely. But, when it is, it is done only in the privacy of the little brown house everyone in Apia visits after lunch or at nights when all the other vendors are asleep. And the pumpkin customers and the peacecorps are asleep, too, in the comfort or discomfort of their small or big-big falepapalagi.

Old men smoke Greys. Young men without money smoke Greys. Greys is raw tobacco too. But, it's one step up from Sa-moan tobacco. Greys tobacco is papalagi tobacco—tamed tobacco, doesn't-bite-your-tongue-off tobacco, doesn't-give-you-bad-breath tobacco...so they say. Greys is distributed in small green boxes, accompanied with their own rolling paper—which made life much easier for Leiloafaikau, the Pancake vendor, who is constantly harrassed for his illiteracy and lack of a public school education...and that he only buys the *Times* just to roll a fag.

Young studs (with or without money) smoke Marlboro, or Rothmans, or cow shit, or weed. Marlboro-Rothmans-Benson— otherwise known as Malapolo-Lafumegi-Pegisoge—are king at the Makeki Fou. They are passed in rows from one pair of lips to the next, sucking in last week's pay (if there was one), sucking in tomorrow's pay (if there is one), sucking, suck-suck until you reach the brown buds and there's no more kau kalo...no more kau fa'i...no more falesamoa...no more paopao...NO MORE NICOTINE!

So you raise cows, or grow weed...or, if you're smart enough, you let someone else raise the cows, let someone else grow the weed. For cow-raising is seriously hard business. Weed growing is seriously hard business, too. Especially if one doesn't have any cows to raise or weed to grow. And when you do have weed to grow there is always that slight chance of trouble from the police...which is sometimes avoidable. The more difficult part in all this is patience. Patience is a gift only a few are blessed with. And the young, with or without cash studs, were out getting pissed when Gabriel was dishing patience out.

Schoolgirls smoke Cool—because they're cool, too—and their

parents don't know it. Nor do any of their relatives or teachers. Schoolgirls wear 'cool' all over their St Mary's College, or Samoa High School, or Pesega College school starched uniforms. All over their teeth, too, especially. They smile a lot at bus drivers, taxi drivers, and young clerks from the Bank of Western Samoa, or from the Public Works…or anyone young and good-looking, and employed somehow.

—

'Employed somehow' is John the Malaefou bus driver, whose birth name is Misiluki Sausaunoa but everyone calls him Johnny—Johnny Boy sometimes because he is the busiest bus driver in the whole of Apia. Johnny Boy is busy and he smokes Malapolo. Johnny Boy is busy and he worships John Wayne.

John Wayne rules his universe. Especially dressed up all cowboy-style, sheriff-style, with a pin on his right breast. John Wayne is cool…next to high-school girls and a playboy pin-up of Miss September, hidden on the bottom of the money box where passengers deposit fares for themselves and their pigs and chickens and fish. Johnny Boy has charm, too. A big smile, too. A big head. And is busy, too…because he has the shortest route a bus could ever wish for and the best music a bus could ever wish for, too. The shortest route hits all the major landmarks in Apia: Beach Road, the clock, the bank, Post Office, reclaimed area, Old Market, Aggie Grey's, Vaisigano, the wharf, Malaefou, Vaiala, Malaetuai, Vaisigano, Aggie Grey's, back to the Maketi-Fou…to the Makeki Fou, blasting the newest 'Islands in the Stream' from Kenny Rogers, blasting Julio Iglesias 'Moonlight Lady,' and an occasional Christmas carol in July.

Johnny Boy wears his charm in Reebok shoes, polyester socks that say 'Addidas' around the ankles, blue shorts, too ('Made in Taiwan'). He has a picture of an eagle fighting a snake with the words: 'You Are My Heart 4–Eva Jane' tattooed into his right arm, below where the arms of his T-shirt end.

Across his right elbow is his social security number: '444–3–T–R–U–S–T–M–E' tattooed in red. His muscles bumping-bumping under music sweat. His muscles bumping-bumping to the teeth of pretty hopeful girls…hopeful because they hope to sit on the seat, next to the busiest bus driver in town, and maybe feel his bumping-bumping American Samoa music muscles.

The clouds in the sky look down at him. They look-look-look with pain. The clouds in the sky are pregnant, too. Rain hasn't visited the town in months. You know this in the way people show their teeth, in the way dogs wag their tails, in the way pulu leaves fall.

—

Pulu leaves have been falling and falling since the last raindrop pissed on cemented Apia. The tree is going slowly bald. Going bald is something sinful in Apia—it is a sin to go bald! Everyone owns such beautiful hair.

Taxis zoom-zoom. Vans zoom-zoom. Lorries zoom-zoom. Bicycles zoom-zoom. Motorcycles zoom-zoom. Tour buses zoom-zoom. A limousine zoom-zooms. Everyone owns a car. Everyone wants to own a car.

At the entrance of the market facing le Fale o Molesi is a big sign in red paint:

Repent! Repent!
17 Years Before
World Comes To End!
Repent! Repent!
Only 144,000 People Welcome
To Gods' Kingdom.
Are You Going To Be Left Out?

—

Fia Agelu—the cool schoolgirl with black mascara on her eye-lashes and five tala and forty sene in her pocket...and member of the Youth For Christ (YFC)—looks up at the sign and says, 'Bless the Lord.'

Fagau Soo—the pulenuu's wife with blue mu'umu'u down to her ankles, and sweat on her forehead, and a child on all ten fingers—looks up at the sign and says, 'Bless the Lord.'

Pau'elo—the layman's prophet–philosopher and pumpkin sell-er, who always wears a black lavalava and never takes showers, and all the children of Savalalo yell out to him, 'Go change into some-thing flowery! This is not some funeral place'—looks up at the sign and says, 'It's gonna be sooner than you think...sooner than you think!'

—

The market is divided into sections. The 'Fruit & Vegetable Section'—which is also the largest section—is made up of pas-sionfruit, esi, banana, guava, avoka, lopa, chinese cabbage, kapisi vai, taro, coconuts, breadfruit, and weed (sold casually between fresh taro leaves). Ulapule and kaulima, and jewelry made from coconut shell and turtle shell and shell from the seashells and nuts, too, make up the smallest section of the market. They are produced 'expertly' by quick fingers and sold quickly, too, to tourists and other Samoans who have no time to produce iekoga-siapo or ula-sisi and are catching the next plane to New Zealand, Australia, or Sweden tomorrow.

—

Dead eels, fish, pigs, octopuses, breadfruit, and bananas are to be found in the 'Food Section'...wrapped around taro leaves, coconut, fresh from the umu.

Imported dead animals like lamb and turkey are also to be found in this section, normally swimming in their own fat...or in the fat of a peanut or sunflower seed or corn. They are sold to hungry customers who rip at the meat, sucking skin and fat, breaking taro or breadfruit, dipping it into the tin plate to absorb more.

'Yummm! Yum,' says Kiai—seven-year-old Kiai Aoga, who skipped school now for the third time this week and is helping his mother finish off a chicken neck in curry.

'Fue ese le lago!' his mother says to him each time flies attack his taro.

—

The 'Pancake Section': flour mixed with salt and water and artificial food colouring, rolled delicately into golf-balls, and dipped into boiling lard.

'Faakau pagikeke! Selling Pancakes! Red pancakes. Blue pancakes. Green pancakes. Banana-filled pancakes, too. Faakau Pagi-keke!'

School children surround this section, handing over whatever money they've been saving just to get a taste of that blue one, of that green one. Chewing-chewing away, they walk with pancakes in their mouths, more pancakes in a brown bag or in newspapers, spotted with fat sieving through.

—

The 'Live Animal Section' is located to the right of the Pancake Section and faces the Development Bank. Octopuses sliver on wet cement. Pigs oink-oink on wet cement. Lobsters attacking the air on wet cement. Crabs attacking lobsters attacking the air on wet cement. Red-yellow-green fish. And more fish. And more pigs and octopuses...slivering and oinking all day long.

—

All day long, too, are young-young studs, flirting with young cool girls in the 'Cool Section'—this can actually be found all over the market. Eyes winking, hands feeling, hands touching breasts (but slightly). It's the...

'Leave me alone!'

'Let's meet again tomorrow...next week?'

'Wanna elope?'

'Wanna suck my dick for five tala?'

section.

—

The 'Taxi Section,' next to the 'Bus Section.'

Bumping, too, out of the taxis is music: rock-and-roll music, modern Samoan music. Modern Samoan music is an electric guitar, and bass, and drums. Unlike old Samoan music where there were perhaps a hundred members in a group: men–women–children…anyone old enough to sing. Singing to the clap of their own hands, or to the beat of a tree trunk, or stones. Modern Samoan music is a band. A band consisting of four or five members, grooving to a Samoanized version of 'Love Me Tender.' Elvis rules! Elvis is alive! Elvis lives in taxis all over Apia—all over Samoa—rock-and-rolling to Samoan lyrics. And Luki the taxi driver turns it up…turns it way up.

Ludwig Spinoza (and everyone calls him Luki), whose great-great-grandfather Heinrich was a colonist (but a good one, his great-great-grandchildren would like us to remember), is a taxi driver. 'He never caused anyone pain' was the logic they gave to justify the goodness of that old man, Heinrich…if you can call impregnating his wife sixteen times (plus three other women from the Yacht Club, plus two house-girls) ecstasy—on his wife's part that is.

He never really oppressed anyone, supressed anyone, or arrested anyone—so his faithful great-great-grandchildren would like us to remember (that is those who care enough to remember). He was a true lover of Samoa—Deutsche Samoa—who loved its women as much as he loved the weather.

Heinrich Spinoza. Herr Spinoza. Mista Sipinosa, as the people of Taufusi came to know him, was a mechanic. He used to fix anything that moved…and in those days that included horses, among other things.

Mista Sipinosa was truly in love with his Samoan wife, Fayawayaway, but he just couldn't keep his pants buttoned when it came to other women—a trait some of his great-great-grandchildren inherited.

But not Luki. Luki is a taxi driver and the closest thing to a mechanic—the only other thing he seemed to have inherited from the dead Mista Sipinosa. Luki the taxi driver is young and married, and has four children. Luki the taxi driver is young and married, and in love with his taxi. You know this by the way he keeps smiling, wetting his upper lip with his tongue each time he looks into the rearview mirror—even when there are no other cars passing. Luki is in love with his taxi…and he takes care of it, too. He washes it, polishes it, looks at it, checks the tyres, the engine, water. And washes it again—three, sometimes nine times a day.

There's a coconut air freshener hanging there right above the mirror. There's a picture of St Joseph standing on a sheep, next to the mirror that says 'Bless This Food, Oh Lord, We Pray,' next to a portrait of Michael Jackson. Christmas balls hang above the radio. A red carpet stretches out on the floor—spotless…not one strand of dirt to be seen.

Luki picks up tourists from the airport every four hours, charging them ten percent above the average rate. That is, if he is in a good mood. Normally he charges twenty percent, sometimes twenty-five—depending on whether or not he had a fight with Le-loomiti that morning.

Luki is the only taxi driver in the whole of Apia who doesn't smoke. There's a red sign that goes on each time a passager steps into the taxi. The red sign says:

Save Your Own Life.
Quit!

—

Dead dogs float on waves. Dead dogs float on waves. They float and float and float on waves. Waves smashing onto rocks. Rocks facing the little brown house everyone visits after lunch. This is the public toilet! Welcome to the 'Public Toilet Section'!

The public toilet is divided into sections—a cartoon of a figure wearing a puletasi to the right and another of a figure in a lava-lava to the left. One can't really distinguish which one is for female and which one is for male…which leads to too much confusion, with most of the male population under 30 or over 75 found 'accidently' in the female section, even though everyone in Apia or from Apia knows that the female section of the little brown house is to the right and that if you were caught accidentally in the 'other' toilet you could easily cover your tracks by saying in a loud voice so that everyone hears:

'I was in a hurry!'

'I didn't know…'

'Things like this happen you know…'

A woman wearing the same smile every day 'on her ear'—that is, a huge aute Samoa smiles some more at you as if she were a clerk at the bank wanting to know if you wanted tens or twenties, but says instead in a very polite voice: 'Peeing or shitting?'

A man dressed in a white iefaikaga (and all the dogs tease him telling him, 'Church is over! Today is Monday, not Sunday') asks you the same question.

'Taking a leak or a dump?'

85

They greet you in their nice manner before you enter the toilet, giving you one round of paper around the palm of their hands if you were taking a leak and two if you were doing heavier work. They'll then say, 'Malo!' or 'Manuia le aso!' if they themselves were having a good day. A bad day being one when the toilets overflowed, or when there wasn't any water and you have to carry your own water from the sea—in a bucket! This happens only rarely.

———

'Did you know Samoa is pregnant?'

'Have you heard the story of the Afega pastor who dropped his lavalava at the Public Works?'

'Ei! Samoa and Samoa eloped last night during the funeral of their grandfather.'

'Samoa was deported from New Zealand last week and is pretending to be on vacation.'

'Samoa the Minister is going to court tomorrow. Eating the sweat of the country.'

'Ai Afu! Did you hear the story of the Afega pastor who dropped his...?'

The 'Gossip Section' (which some prefer to call the 'storytelling section' or 'talk-story section') like the Cool Section, is to be found all over the market. Then there is the 'Comedy Section.' Someone slipping on a banana peel landing on their arm or leg or nose is the comedy section (not the agony section). Someone slipping on the same banana peel cracking their skin or skull is the comedy section (not the tragic section). All sections connected somehow by tobacco smoke, guava hearts, love notes, bank notes, fish scales, burnt lard…and pregnant pumpkins.

Besides hanging from the sky, pumpkins are sold in the food section. Pumpkins are baked whole in an umu, sometimes with coconut milk and a dead fish swimming there in complete orangeness. Sometimes taro leaves are picked instead, and wrapped in coconut milk and left growing in the orangeness… surrounded, too, by hot stones earth and fire…ventilated by banana leaves. Pumpkin buds are gathered by children in a basket and taken to their mothers who wash them and drop them in a soup. Pumpkin seeds are roasted too. The seeds opened and eaten. Sometimes traded for marbles or hairpins.

—

'The Spirit of '76' attaches itself in large capital letters to the T-shirt of an important looking man. The important looking man is the Head of Personnel at Le Fale o Molesi, one of the few department store giants in Apia. The man is sitting on a bench at the food section, sucking his fingers, licking his fingers, savouring turkey arse fat. The fat crawls slowly down to his elbows…swimming-swimming, too, on a tin plate ladden with taro and coconut milk, and onions and flies.

The flies buzz-buzz each time the man rips flesh from bone. He throws the bone to the floor, to a one-eyed dog who picks it up with his teeth and sends it as a present to his liver.

Filiga Filiga, Head of Personnel at Le Fale o Molesi, is on his lunch break. He doesn't like eating at the Makeki Fou, but it's the only alternative. It's the only place where a Samoan can still eat like a Samoan without paying papalagi prices. Filiga wishes sometimes to eat once at a restaurant. But he can't. He is too much of a family man. One course at a restaurant and he feeds his wife and their children. Two meals at a restaurant and you feed a mistress, her cousins, and the whole 'aiga. This is Filiga's logic—the price he has to pay for breathing in dead dogs on waves and shit from the little big house the whole of Apia visited after lunch…

He knows the price he has to pay, too, for constantly meeting (with no initiation on his behalf) relatives from kua-back or Savai'i who always gave him that look, that 'you're the Head of the Personnel Department at Le Fale o Molesi and we're still in the plantations, weeding-weeding' look. Then they'll go on to say, in the humblest of voices,

'Se ka tu!'

'I have a little fa'alavelave.'

'My youngest daughter died and we're in Apia looking for a coffin.'

'Spare a cigarette? Thirty sene? Se ka pasese?'

'I should start eating at a restaurant,' he mumbles under the flies on his tin plate. 'Maybe I should…maybe.'

Each meal at the Makeki Fou leads to this 'maybe–maybe' rhetoric.

—

'Water is Life,' says the sign on the tyres of a government van. 'Conserve water in Samoa.'

Samoa was founded in 1962.

Samoa is founded on god. E fa'avae Samoa i le Atua.

Not the mid. Not the centre.

Not the womb of Laueleele.

Not the Tuli. Not the Pili.

Not the conch shell. Not the Owl.

Not the Octopus. Not the Eel.

Not the conch shell. Not the Owl.

Not the Sea. Not the… Not the…

Not the god. Not the god.

Samoa is founded on the 'Not the' god.

The new god.

The very hungry god—hungrier than the biggest shark, hungrier than the biggest moon. The new god is hungry and big, and is everywhere and nowhere, too. Unlike the old gods, who needed the sea, or the sky, or the darkness of a cave, or the intimacy of a malumalu built to house them, the new god is housed in big, extravagant falesa, decorated with clocks, books and plastic flowers. Each village has one…sometimes four…sometimes nine.

A woman is walking towards the Fale o Molesi. There is a baby bundled in faded lavalava under her arms. The baby is silent. Silent. The woman feels the heat of tar under the skin of her feet. She walks barefoot. She walks with pride, too. Pride too, because she is meeting the Head of Personnel of Le Fale o Molesi. The Head of Personnel of Le Fale o Molesi planted his seed in her daughter's womb, and left. Now she was here…here with the bundle, here with the flower blooming–blooming…the flower come to claim her branch, her leaves, her roots.

'I am a relative,' says Su'ekage. 'I'm here with a message for Filiga. It is very important.'

Clerk (all decorated Christmas-like): 'But he is in a meeting with the pule o Molesi. It is impossible for us to reach him at the moment.'

Fiakagaka (holding onto the crying-crying baby pissing onto

her only good lavalava, trying to ignore the screaming thing, trying to look proud in her bare feet.): 'Then we will wait.'

'Suit yourselves,' says Mrs Claus. 'Goddamned kua-backs!'

Mrs Santa Claus, the clerk, in her high-heel shoes and red-red lips and pearly earrings and skin-tight dress and shocking pink claws and 'I Love You Forever' gold-chain gilded around her neck, steps back into the booth where she is imprisoned, counting-counting. One tala, two tala, ten tala…a hundred and nine. Her lips moving-moving. Her eyes moving-moving. Her fingertips moving, too. Flies zoom-zoom by, buzz around her nose, buzz around her ears, sitting on the 'I Love You Forever' gold-chain lovely around her neck. She waves the flies away. The flies wave back at her, at the dirty paper-money slipping-slipping between her fingertips.

—

Night.

Darkness.

Night falls and falls on the market, and the market is silent, and the sections are all closed. In the dark women and men sleep on mats on the cement. These are the women and men who didn't sell much during daylight, and didn't have bus fare to return home. One of them is Mataolepo—eye of the night—or Po, or Mata as some of her relatives call her.

Po is sitting in the dark on a mat on the cement of the Makeki Fou. She is looking out to the lights of the Tusitala Hotel. Tusitala was the name nineteenth-century Samoans gave the tuberculosis stricken Scottish writer Robert Louis Stevenson, who once lived in the biggest house in the whole of Samoa and had servants to cook for him, and to sing to him, and to make him and Fanny 'paradise happy,' and wiped his sick arse, too...and hers, too, whenever it was needed. Tusitala means 'writer of stories' in English, or 'a Japanese-owned hotel'...depending on who's doing the translation or defining.

And Po looks on...looks on and on...smoking tobacco wrapped around the front page of the *Times*.

POEM OF PISA

Between Fiakagaka's fingers a cigarette was burning as we waited.

Wait. Wait. We waited. Me, pissing over and over. Fiakagaka changing me but once.

'That's the last cloth,' she said, loud enough for Mrs Claus to raise an eyebrow and look.

Feet passed us sitting there in front of Le Fale o Molesi.

Cars honked horns.

Lorries honked horns.

Buses honked, too.

Cigarette buds flick–flicked on the cement.

Ashes.

More cigarette buds.

We waited.

Waited still for the man.

—

Le Kamaloa, as Pisa's people referred to Filiga.

Le Tamaloa, as Fiakagaka kept repeating and repeating each

time I cried or shat or pissed.

'He's going to make you a daughter. He's going to make your mother a wife—respectable in the eyes of god, the village, the 'aiga. He's gonna give you life,' mumbled Fiakagaka in my small-small ears.

We waited for him. Him, the man.

Him, the saviour. Waited.

Waited. Waited until a siren roared through the streets of Apia and it was four o'clock. Everything was to be closed:

Public Works, NPF,

Bank of Western Samoa,

Post Office, Fale o Amau,

Fale o Pipi, Fale Talavai,

Nelson Library, Fale o Molesi...

everything—except the Makeki Fou.

—

A large man with papalagi shoes, pants, and uniform matching shirt is walking towards a large woman with Christmas decorations. She wears palagi shoes, handbag, red lips, fake-gold earrings, fake-gold necklace, gold wedding ring around fat fingers, watch around the wrist, each wrist attached to a little girl—one about ten; the other, seven.

Both girls are wearing blue sandals, blue uniforms, and blue ribbons on their braided hair, and big smiles on their faces.

'Papa! Papa!' they cry in unison.

One of the girls runs over to the man, and the man picks her up and throws her gently into the air.

The girl's smile turns to a big laugh...and she laughs and laughs and laughs some more.

'Where's my lollies? Where's my Twisties? Where's my pencil-case? Where's my pencils…?'

The man puts both of his hands into each pocket and produces four lollipops, two bags of chicken flavoured Twisties, a red pencil-case, three red pencils and three blue ones. He divides them between the two little girls, giving the pencil-case to the younger girl. On receiving these gifts they dance and dance around in circles.

'We have lollipops. We have Twisties… We have lollipops. We have Twisties…'

'Shhhhhhhhh,' says the woman.

'Not so loud,' says the woman.

The girls dance and dance, deaf to the voice of the woman.

'I have to go get my things,' says the man to the woman. 'It won't take long.'

—

Dance, dance…the girls continue dancing.
Licking the redness of lollipop sweetness.
Sucking on the sugar of lollipop sweetness.
Their eyes full of joy.
Their tongues red like fire.

—

Fifteen minutes pass on the watch on the fat wrist of the very patient, fake gold-necklaced, flaming red-lipped woman.

Thirty minutes pass on the watch of the now chain-smoking, tired-looking, very impatient woman.

94

'Where the hell is your father?' says the woman to the little girls...the little girls sitting on the cement in front of Le Fale o Molesi.

No more lollipop faces.

No more big smile faces.

Teeth now full of boredom.

They bow their heads to ants crawling on the cement.

They bow their ears, too, to the voice of their mother.

'How are we supposed to know?' they wish to say, but keep their opinions whispered...loud enough for only ants to hear.

'One of you girls, go to the back there and ask Lita or Jane where your father is.'

The girls continue to not listen, continue indulging in their own boredom.

'I said *now!* Bake you in an oven!' hisses the woman.

—

The older girl stands up from the cement, dusts the back of her uniform and starts walking, head down still, towards the back of the Fale o Molesi. Jane, the Head Accountant and personal long-time friend of the woman, sees her from a distance and calls to her.

'What are you doing here? Your father left an hour ago.'

'But we've been waiting...'

'He said he was going to Savai'i and that your mother already knew. Didn't you know?'

'I didn't...that he...my mother and my sister are...'

Blackness.

Everything black.

Jane the Head Accountant, black.

The blue bricks on the side wall of the Fale o Molesi, black.

Cars zooming by, black.

Clouds, black.

Sky, black.

Everything.

'Auoi ka fefe!' says Jane the Head Accountant, just before she sees the ten-year-old body collapse onto the floor.

'Help! Help!'

The Christmas-decorated woman and the bored little girl in the front of the Fale o Molesi hear Jane the Head Accountant cry and rush to the back of the building—the little girl running-running faster than the woman, the woman nearly falling off the heels of her high-high shoes, Rothmans attached still to her fingers.

Before the woman can open her mouth to ask what has happened, her eyes catch sight of Jane the Head Accountant, Lita the Clerk, and a few other female clerks hovering over the body of the little girl. She rushes over to the other women, waves them all away, and orders someone to fetch water.

'Don't just stand there, you stupid bitches! Get some water!'

Because she is the wife of the Head of Personnel, and because she is very very big and powerful, and known throughout Apia (because of the many faces she has rearranged), feet scattered and bodies scattered with them, returning like lightning with water in bottles…even in bowls. The woman dips the end of her floral skirt into the bowl of water, rinses it, and presses the cool material onto the forehead of the still-unconscious girl.

An eyelid moves.

More coolness on the forehead.

Both eyelids moving.

More movement.

More coolness. Brightness (slowly).

The little little girl looks up into the faces of the women staring down at her little-brightened face.

'Are you alright?' the women chorus in high soprano.

'What happened?' mumbles the little little girl. 'What happened?'

—

Five days later, on a Saturday afternoon, Filiga returned suddenly to Malaefou. He wore a black lavalava, a white shirt and was bare-foot. There was a baby in his arms.

All the children of Malaefou rushed to him as soon as he exited the bus and started following him towards his house, asking him if he could give them money for the snow-cone man and where did he get that baby?

The baby looked at the children and gave out a big cry. Filiga patted her on the back while reaching into his iefaikaga, pulling out whatever loose change he had there, then throwing them out to the children…who ran after the coins, fighting and shouting.

Filiga entered the house.

Tausi, his seventy-year-old mother, was sitting on the cement floor weaving a fan. Logo was sitting in the back of the house, searching for lice in the hair of the fully conscious, previously (five days ago) unconscious, elder girl.

'Papa! Papa!' cried the little girl. 'Papa!'

'Go and play,' said Filiga to the girl. 'Take your sister with you.'

The little girl, unaccustomed to her papa's new voice, fled to the back of the fale where her mother was sitting, lice between her lips.

'I've taken a new wife,' said Filiga to the rest of the family, not looking at Logo. 'Tell the "woman" to leave the house *today.* Leave the girls behind. Let her pack her things and leave. I don't want to see her in this house again. *Ever!'*

Silence.

Five minutes passed on the watch on the wrist of the woman sitting there, on the table with lice residue between her lips.

Complete silence. The complete silence that falls before a storm.

Logo stood up slowly, went into the room where they kept the pusa and the bed, and all their belongings.

'Auoi ka fia ola!' she screamed. 'What have I done wrong? What is this all about? Tell me! Tell me, Tausi! Have I ever failed to take care of you the way you are accustomed? Have I ever failed to put food on your plate, wash your clothes, iron your clothes, praise you in public...?'

Logo was pulling her hair out, ripping the framed pictures of her and her daughters off the walls. Her voice rose higher and higher, while women and children, and men and dogs were peeping in through the louvres.

'Go get Lafoga!' Lafoga the pastor, who was always troubled from his breakfast, lunch, or dinner whenever the lambs of God needed to be rescued from a valley, a hill, or from themselves.

Everyone was curious. Everyone was hungry, too, for blood.

'Is Filiga going to beat up Logo before he kicks her out of the house?'

'Is he going to even kill her?'

Their curiosity (and hopes) evaporated when they saw Filiga exiting the fale with the baby still in his arms. Minutes before Lafoga arrived with a chicken leg stuck still to his nose. Filiga exited, embarrassed.

'Escaped!' the lament of the woman who bore him two little girls, ironed his clothes for the last five years of marriage in front of God and the people of Malaefou, cooked his food, supervised his village affairs, knew of all the secrets (besides the women) that lived in his heart, knew of his wanting to be pulenuu of Malaefou even though he didn't have an important matai title, knew of his wanting to lead the Au Faipese malaga to New Zealand even though he wasn't the kaikaipese, knew of his wanting to be the first to play the electrical organ the church was getting in three months time, knew of his fear of losing his job, of his wanting to...

—

Logo's voice flew higher and higher, flying out through the louvres, uniting with the salt-breeze, floating-floating towards the pastor's house, past the graves, past the pulu tree, past the malae, past the church.... Logo's voice carried with it the weight of her suffering—her pained skin, which she scratched and scratched with her own fingernails; her lovely hair, partly bald in the front after she pulled and pulled...

The family belongings were scattered all over the room.

But most evident of all was her anger, anger not at Filiga but at the source—the woman causing all this pain.

Tausi, her slowly-going-deaf seventy-year-old mother-in-law

who heard only the scratches Logo made on her skin, put the fan she was weaving aside and moved her body toward the room where her daughter-in-law was crying. Logo saw Tausi's feet moving toward her on the wooden floor and she started singing once more.

'Tell me...tell me, Tausi! Have I ever...?'

The old woman bent down and put her loose arms around the younger woman. Logo refused at first, but then held on tightly to Tausi, as if they were welcoming each other for the first time.

'Logo, patience. Logo, patience. Logo, onosaʻi' was all Tausi managed to say to comfort her.

'I'm going to kill her,' said Logo. 'I'm going to return the pain she's caused by ripping out her throat and baking her pig-body in a umu...'

'Logo, patience....'

—

That night found Logo and Tausi asleep in the darkness of the little room, belongings scattered everywhere.

Filiga returned neither that evening nor the next...or the next.

On the third evening, he entered the fale again to find the little room empty—no Logo, none of her clothes, none of *his* good Sunday clothes, no pusa, no nothing, but the girls. The girls were still there, laughing with their cousins as if nothing ever happened.

—

A week after Logo left, rumour had it she bought a ticket and went by boat to American Samoa, where she found a job working at the fish factory, and a half-Korean half-Samoan man to help forget Filiga and the pain of the other woman, whom she vowed she would kill if she ever returned to Malaefou.

—

Then Pisa appeared on the steps of the Filiga fale with the baby bundled in her hands, wrapped in newspapers.

No one noticed her at first—that is to say, no adults were there to see her, only children. They teased her that she was poor, and that she wore no sandals, and that her feet were all cracked, and that her clothes didn't match, and that she wrapped her baby in the *Samoa Times,* and that she had holes in her lavalava.... And where did she come from? The boat?

Pisa told the children to go eat shit—all of them—and that they had no manners.

The children mocked Pisa.

'You go eat shit, you stranger...you strange, strange woman with the strange, strange baby and the strange, strange smell. Go drown yourself in the tide, too, while you're at it.' The children yelled back at her until evening fell.

A crowd of teenage girls gathered around the breadfruit tree on the right side of the Filiga fale. The teenage girls were looking at the woman rocking the very silent baby in her lap. Flies were swimming on the eyelids of the little baby and the woman let them. The girls laughed and giggled, and laughed until they were sprayed suddenly by a shower of pebbles and obscenities.

'Get out of there, you faikakala.' It was a male voice. It was the voice of Asu, Filiga's youngest unmarried brother.

Asu told the sitting Pisa to bring the baby into the house.

'Tausi, his mother, requests it.'

'But I am not…I will enter only when Filiga returns and tells me to enter his family's fale.'

She would wait some more…she waited…waiting…

—

The conch shell is blown, but the woman sits quite still with the baby crying–crying now.

Mosquitoes settle on the baby's toes, neck, and eyelids.

'Tell the "woman" to come in!' It was a female voice, clearly the voice of Tausi.

'Tell the woman to bring my grandchild into the house!'

On hearing this Pisa stood up, her feet tired, her feet forgetting how to walk. Darkness fell and kept falling until Pisa took her first step into the Filiga fale.

'How shameful!' was the greeting she got as soon as she stepped into the fale.

'How shameful!' said Tausi again when she saw the newspaper bundle. 'Do you not have shame? How dare you wrap my grand-child in a newspaper? How dare you? Do you think you're still in Savai'i? What do you think everyone is going to be talking about? That the Filiga 'aiga cannot afford cotton? That the Filiga 'aiga is poor? You have to understand one thing if you're going to live under this fale: never wrap my grandchild in newspaper again. Do you understand?'

Pisa—tired and anxious to see Filiga, embarrassed by Tausi and the other women of the 'aiga—bowed her head, shook it side to side and said in a very low voice, 'Yes, I understand.'

Loto and Sisila, Logo's children, ran over to the bundle and started stroking it. Pisa looked down at the two little girls and saw

Filiga in their eyes…and became sick. She excused herself and left the fale with the bundle, then threw up all of that morning's tea…threw up all of her self. Looking onto the paepae of the fale, she saw her life and she knew that she was dead. She was already dead the moment the thing screamed its first scream. She looked into the eyes of the thing, and started crying and crying and crying…until the all-powerful female voice of Tausi was heard again.

'Tell her to bring the girl in the house…! Crying like a fool out there in the night. Who's ever heard of such a thing? Crying like a fool out there in the night. What does she think this is? A school? Papauka? You should have known better before you… Ah! What's the use? Leave the girl here, and go in the back and help the women with the fire…go in the back and help the women with the fire…help the women with the fire…with the fire…the fire…fire.'

—

Fire. That's where she would have to spend the rest of her life, in the fire, next to the fire.

'Mu ou maka i le afi.'

'Burn your eyes in the fire.'

For that is what happened to any woman who eloped and lived with the man's 'aiga. That is what happened to every woman who had to replace a wife or (in this case) wives.

She was compared constantly to the second wife…not to the first wife, as if the first wife never existed.

Logo never made tea that was asua.

Logo made the best koko alaisa in the whole of Malaefou.

'Do you remember how she would wake up at six every

morning to prepare the old lady's food?'

'Do you remember how her family would come from Savai'i with pigs and taro and bananas if our family ever had a faalavelave? How her children were spotless. Clean. Not one sore on their bodies. Not one uku in their hair. There's a good woman for ya!'

'There's a good woman for ya!'

'But men are sometimes like that. Bake them in an oven! Why isn't one woman enough?'

'Why did he have to go all the way to Savai'i to come back with this…this…this pulali…kao i se umu!'

Pisa knew they were talking about her—all this in front of her, all this to annoy her, humiliate her. Every time she didn't please someone, words would fly out of their mouths; like poisonous fish they flew. They flew out of their mouths and attacked her eyes. They flew out of their mouths and attacked her ears, her feet, her fingernails, her tongue.

'Why don't they just beat me up, if that's what they want?' she asked herself. 'Why didn't they just do that, instead of all the words?'

—

Sometimes they did beat her up.

They threw shoes at her eyes if her baby was found pissing on the old lady's bed. They pulled her hair and slapped her mouth if the curry was too salty or the tea was too sweet.

Her own mouth did not exist in those early days—it didn't. It didn't have a voice. It didn't even have sound. Her mouth only grunted in agreement with someone over how brilliant the Filiga family was in some way—only in agreement with someone over how rich the Filiga family was, and how every family member in New Zealand contributed to the pastor's plate every month, every Children's Sunday, every Christmas.

She nodded her head every time someone praised the Filiga children and grandchildren for how smart they were, how they always came first place in the Aoga a le Faifeau and Aoga Aso Sa, how they performed the best play on every Children's Sunday.

Pisa nodded her head at Tausi's mat weaving, or fan weaving, or character. She nodded her affirmation that Tausi was the best mother-in-law any daughter-in-law could ever ask for, that she was not only kind but fair. She gave you sheets and pillowcases to start your family. She beat you up if her son wasn't there… because she loved you and because she wanted to teach you how to be a member of the Filiga clan. Tausi was old, but still strong. Tausi was old, but still had all her mea-faigaluega with her— meaning, she could still rearrange your face if you asked for it.

Pisa was helpless—hopeless, even. And so young—she was twenty years younger than the second wife! She was just a kid— eighteen, with hopes of getting a scholarship and going to New Zealand.

How could she know she was going to be seduced by a middle-aged man who was not a matai or head of any clan as he had led her to believe?

Or that she was going to carry his child?

Or that it was going to be a girl and she would burn her eyes in the fire until the end of her days?

How could she know that the man was married and that he already had two little girls…and two wives…and that one of them committed suicide?

He told her he wasn't married, didn't have a wife, didn't have children. He told her that he was in Savai'i working for himself and his 'aiga—meaning, his mother, brothers and sisters, their husbands and wives, their children.

He wasn't married. He swore it.

—

And the moon didn't help things either.

And the wind didn't help things either.

The moon. The wind.

The wind. The child.

How did she know that one, only one poke would lead to a child?

And a female at that?

—

This fact alone made her realize that she was truly cursed...that she was cursed, just like her mother, to bear girls. This was the tradition in her 'aiga. This was the curse of girls. Girls would grow up and continue the cycle of being seduced by middle-aged men. Girls would grow up to shame their 'aiga and to burn their eyes in the fire.

'Why?' she asked herself, as she scraped skin from taro, from breadfruit...dropping them into boiling water...squeezing coconut milk through a kauaga...waiting until the saka was cooked then adding the salted coconut milk...frying elegi in onions and beans...serving them on tin plates and a laulau...serving them to the old lady and to the women of the family who all sat in the front, at the head of the fale, waiting.

Waiting for their chance to compare, waiting for their chance to criticize—even when Filiga was there. His sisters (addressed more commonly as *the* sisters), 'noble and big and immobile,' and 'noble and skinny and immobile,' would complain for the third night in a row that the koko Samoa was not sweet enough…or that the faalifu fa'i was not salted and lacked onions.

Tausi, too, would mumble something under her breath. When Filiga asked her what it was she wanted to say, it was, 'nothing, nothing.'

She said this in such a way that one could not help but ask her again, and again—which Filiga always did.

'Nothing.'

And Filiga would reply not so much in defence of Pisa, but in appeasement.

'Soia ia, she's young. She'll learn.'

'Learn to what?' Pisa asked herself after overhearing this. 'Learn to what? To salt the coconut milk fifty different ways in order to please every single person in the fale? To sugar the koko alaisa fifty different ways to please every single person in the fale? To do this, to do that fifty different ways to…'

—

These early days were filled with tears, pools of them. One could practically go fishing in the sea of tears Pisa cried. She found herself weeping constantly at nights when Filiga and the whole of the 'aiga were sleeping, and she was the only one awake…awake.

These are the moments, too, when she thought of Vaisola, the first wife—Vaisola with the dead womb. No one ever knew that she was thinking of Vaisola. She never told anyone. No one ever asked. She thought of Vaisola in the same situation, in the same fale as Tausi, in the same fale as Tausi's daughters. Did she, too, burn her eyes in the fire? Have to salt the faalifu fa'i fifty different ways? Have shoes thrown at her face because her baby peed on the bed?

'Of course not!' Pisa would mumble. 'Of course not!'

Could she say then, that Vaisola was lucky she didn't have shoes dancing on her eyelids whenever the baby urinated on the bed?

But Vaisola didn't have a baby. She may have had to burn her eyes in the fire or be insulted because the koko Samoa was not sugared correctly, but she didn't have shoes flying her way. Besides, Filiga was married to her. That was a big difference between them. In addition, Vaisola came from a good family— meaning they had a title the size of the universe, and a plantation and pigs to support that universe. Therefore she couldn't have possibly been mistreated by the sisters or by Tausi.

Why then?

———

So many questions. At that moment all rhetorical, for no one in the family cared to talk about Vaisola. Her name was never mentioned. It died along with her feet, like her dead womb that refused to produce anything...so nothing was remembered.

———

Pisa heard the sound of a ve'a crying but once through Malaefou. This was the sign of death, the death of a family member far away or the death of someone near. This scared her and she moved closer to Filiga, avoiding his snores. It was during these moments that she was forced to look at the man she had eloped with.

She tried not to understand too much of him: the way he thought, why he liked other women, and why he left them. For the moment all she saw was a husband—minus his first wife, minus his second wife, minus his children. She thought once more about what her mother said to her just before she left her at the wharf.

'What makes you think he's gonna stay with you?'

'He will,' she remembered answering stubbornly. 'I'll make him. After all, he was the one who came to my village.'

He had been quiet and humble, too, asking her father if they could live together—actually wanting the baby, even though it was a girl. He must love her...he must.

Pisa did not know what to think. She had been thinking all night, all night without end, thinking-thinking-thinking that he must love her, however he defined it. Whether that meant appeasing his mother, his sisters, the 'aiga—these were surely all signs of his alofa which he never verbally expressed to her in public or in private.

She thought that perhaps she loved him back, too...stroking his hair in the middle of the night while he slept, stroking his face in the middle of the night while he slept. She felt protected by his presence. She was willing to go through whatever pain, whatever insults to hold onto him. She could change him and help him change himself. Maybe one day he would marry her in church for all of Malaefou to see...for all of Malaefou to know that she, Pisa Tutulu, was a somebody worthy of marriage; that she, Pisa Tutulu, although she came from a poor, unimportant family from

Savai'i, was now a confirmed member of the Filiga family and a married wife of one of the sons of the Filiga clan. Although he was not an important matai himself, Filiga was at least the Head of Personnel at Le Fale o Molesi. People would no longer refer to her as 'the woman.' Rather, they would address her properly, as Filiga's married wife.

These were Pisa's last thoughts as she drifted off to sleep.

A GOOD MAN

Mr Brown loved a lot with his fingers and tongue, not his penis, said Lili suddenly one evening…as we did what we usually did on evenings when there was no meeting of any kind—sitting under the pulu, singing songs, counting stars, and telling stories. Moa and I looked at each other uneasily.

'What are you talking about?'

'Sing louder,' she said, 'so that no one can hear us.'

'Tuli mai, tuli mai
tuli mai, tuli mai—
tuli mai, le aitu ma le sauai a maua e ai—
tatou sosola ia, o le a sau le loomatua—
faapea ma le toeaina e fulufulua le papa tua—
aue! aue!
aue! aue!
aue, lo'u loto e ua le moe—
talu lo'u fia vaai—
fuga ia oe—

talu lo'u fia faitama e maua ai ita i nuu ese…
tuli mai, tuli…'

'What do you mean?' we asked again after we finished the third song.

All we knew about sex or anything related to it came from Lili. She was the one who told us how to wrap a safe, how to avoid cold showers during the moon's visit, how to avoid winkers (by pretending you're not interested, even if you were), how to choose the right bra, how to smoke a cigarette (swallow the smoke).

'Mr Brown doesn't have a penis,' she said, looking towards the sea. 'But he looks like a man, doesn't he?'

'He fooled me,' said Moa, shaking her head in confusion.

'It doesn't work! It hasn't worked for years. Maybe he used it too much when he was young, or maybe a woman sucked all the mana out of it. Who knows? He was with me this afternoon…and you better not repeat this to anyone, especially your cousin Pepe. Today he came home for afternoon meal and I was in the shower cleaning. I knew he was in the shower-room watching me, but I didn't say anything. Maybe I wanted him to…to watch me cleaning…to watch me…to watch. Maybe I've always wanted to do it with a palagi…any palagi.

'Then Mr Brown whispered very suddenly, very softly: "Sheila …my little Samoan Sheila."

'When I looked back he wasn't there and I thought maybe it was a dream. Maybe I thought too much about Mr Brown…and I was hearing things I shouldn't be hearing…things I couldn't be hearing.

112

'Then I heard sobs. Someone was crying. Someone was crying-crying. And I went out of the shower-room to look. I found Mr Brown naked on his bed. He was crying. I was sad for Mr Brown. I was afraid, too, because I've never seen a man cry—except at funerals. I thought one of Mr Brown's relatives was dead and that he was crying for them, and that this was the way palagis lamented.

'"Oh, my little Samoan Sheila," he kept mumbling over and over.

'He looked up to me standing there...me who was looking down at his naked crying body...and he opened his arms to me.

'"Come," he said waving. I forgot my head where I was standing and my hands started moving on their own...slowly removing my clothes. I wanted to comfort him you see...the way I comforted Ike when his father died. So I took off my panties and went into Mr Brown's arms.

'He kissed my breasts first...then my mouth...then my breasts again...then my stomach. Then he told me to turn around to the back and he kissed my back, starting from my neck all the way to my feet. He put each toe into his mouth and sucked them as if they were lollipops. His fingers played and played with the hair. Then he spread my legs apart and buried his head where his fingers played.

'"I'm ready, Mr Brown," I said.

'And that's when he started crying again...and that's when I looked at him and saw the reason for his lament. His penis was dead. It lay there wrinkled like a rain-worm...all curled up... afraid of the sun.

'I wiped the tears from Mr Brown's eyes and put them in my

own mouth…and I pushed Mr Brown's head back down to the hair and whispered to him.

'"Sheila is here, Mr Brown. Little Samoan Sheila is here."'

—

Lili was crying when she finished the story about Mr Brown. She was loving Mr Brown and Mr Brown didn't take her with him to Australia. Mr Brown said that Lili wouldn't be happy living in Australia…that she would be better off in Samoa…which Moa and I still don't understand.

'There's no 'aiga in Australia,' said Mr Brown.

'But I don't want 'aiga,' said Lili.

'You're never going to make an 'aiga with me, Ma'alili.' That was the first time Mr Brown called Lili by her full name…ever.

'I don't want 'aiga. I already have a…'

'I want you to be happy. That's why I'm not taking you…I'm not taking you…I'm not…not.'

—

Before Mr Brown left he made a bank account for Lili at the Bank of Western Samoa and left five hundred tala in it, and he enrolled Lili at the typing school at Lalovaea. He left three pairs of shoes for Lili's brothers…plus all the food and kitchenware and garden supplies and everything else he didn't take with him. He sold my 'aiga the transformer and antennae, which ended weeks of shame we went through from villagers who kept teasing us about our broken TV and our un-rich New Zealand relatives.

'He was a good man,' Moa and I said in unison to Lili, who was wiping the tears from her eyes with the end of her lavalava.

'Yeah, yeah,' she mumbled.

'If he's so good, where is he now?' she wanted to say.

But she didn't. She knew he was a good man...she knew it and we knew it, too. He was the only man who ever loved her. He was the only man *she* ever loved.

MEMORY

We were terrified of dreams. Death lived in dreams. So we avoided them, everyone did. Aitu roamed around at night, listening to people tell dreams, watching people tell dreams. Whenever someone had a bad dream, they wouldn't tell anyone about it. No one told a dream in the dark, only women in a group, in a circle.

When the evening meal was eaten and there was no Aufaipese, and no Aukalavou, and the electricity bill was not paid so that we couldn't watch TV, and the women of the house were tired enough to not take notice of us girls sitting in on their nightly conversations, they told the story of Fa'afetai's birth and the death of Alofa.

This is before any of us girls was born. This is when the household was much smaller. Tausi's husband and our grandfather, Esau Filiga, was alive still, and only eight of their thirteen children were married and had children (our cousins).

Alofa was the youngest of Tausi's thirteen children. She was said to be very beautiful, and a matai from Savai'i who was a friend of Esau's wanted to marry her.

She, in turn, did not want to marry the matai. She was seventeen. He was forty-two. She wanted to go to New Zealand and was in love with a palagi, Dr Epson. Dr Epson worked at Motootua National Hospital. Alofa helped him in the room where babies were born.

Tausi dreamt Alofa's death was everyone's conclusion after Alofa died. Like Fa'afetai, she too drowned, her soul snatched by hungry waves, waves that appeared and kept appearing in Tausi's Lightness...for to dream is to go back to the Lightness, back to before.

'Before what?' we girls would ask.

'Don't ask,' old people would say. 'Don't ask.'

Tausi dreamt and dreamt and dreamt...always about Alofa getting married, but not in a church. Alofa would marry a man without a face, she said. They would sail out to sea in a canoe, and they would throw flowers and ula pua to eels who would come to the surface of the sea and greet only Alofa to her new home.

'You will leave your 'aiga to go live with your husband. This is where your husband comes from. We are his 'aiga,' the eels said.

Tausi always woke up when Alofa stepped out of the canoe and into a falesamoa...and there was a fono in the falesamoa, and all the matai were octopus, magigi, malau, sharks, and eels.

The faipele told our women that the dream didn't mean anything because the same things happen over and over...and, according to Tausi, Alofa's feet never touched the sea, they touched the paepae of the falesamoa each time she steps out of the canoe.

'If she touches the sea,' said the faipele, 'then one of you is going to die. If she touches the paepae then another one of you is going to be born.'

A year went by after Tausi's wedding dreams stopped visiting her. Fa'afetai was born to Fale and Motu'ese.

Alofa was found hanging from Room 211 at Motootua National Hospital. People said she wanted to cheat her mother's dream. She wanted to take her own life before someone else did. Other people said un-returned alofa from Dr Epson—who had a Mrs Epson and three afakasi kids—was the someone else that made Alofa hang herself. Some say still that Tausi was lying in the telling of her dream and that Alofa's feet did touch the sea.

'Why doesn't she tell the truth?' women asked each other.

'She's going to live a long life,' one women said of Tausi. 'She is afraid of Death, and Death is afraid of her. She is going to live and live and live…'

—

I think sometimes about Alofa and how beautiful she must have been, and how, despite her death and in spite of Tausi's conspiracy (if there was one), and in spite of how everyone talks of love only when they talk-story about her, I realise deep down that I hate her and that I despise her legacy, which is my legacy also.

I am named Alofa to keep her alive, so that when people call my name they call hers. But I am ugly; I am not beautiful. I am not comparable to the dirt in her once alive toenails. I am nothing.

Sometimes people say, it's just a waste of Alofa's name on me. I don't act at all like her. I am lazy…and cheeky and ugly…an in-between. Not beautiful at all, like Alofa makua. They wish they'd call me something else. I wish sometimes that she did not die, and that she would live and live, and be old and get fat, and get ugly, too.

Why didn't Dr Epson love her back? Did he love her back, and maybe Mrs Epson found out and threatened to kill her...so that she committed her own death out of fear? Did she feel the same way Lili feels about Mr Brown? Is Lili going to hang herself, too, one day?

But Mr Brown is gone, I assure myself. Mr Brown is gone... and Fa'afetai is gone...and Alofa is gone, too...and Lili is here... and I am here.

I am Alofa's memory. I live so that she does not die.

Will she die when I die? Will someone else be named Alofa when I die, so that old Alofa and me, young Alofa, don't die?

FEAR OF THE MOON

Before I finally got the moon sickness and before the moon even knew that I existed, I was terrified all through Form Two and Form Three.

'Girls who don't get it before they're seventeen die,' Moa and Lili said. 'We know of someone from St Mary's College who was eighteen and died suddenly while she was swimming in the sea. Some people said she was fasia, because she was too beautiful. But, women say she died because the moon forgot her.'

Girls who didn't get it and lived would never find husbands. No one wanted someone who was forgotten by the moon. Girls who didn't get it but lived would never be able to carry a baby in their womb, even if they did 'it' with a sailor or someone who wasn't going to marry them.

Sometimes I cut my own fingers and dripped blood onto a self-made safe and stuck it in my crotch. When it was shower time in the evening, I would take the safe out and say, 'Look! I got it! The moon remembered!'

Sometimes, too, I would think about the girl from St Mary's College, and I wondered: 'If beautiful girls died from it, then how is the moon going to treat someone like me?'

I imagined the St Mary's College girl being just as terrified as I was. Maybe she knew it was time for her to die. No one goes swimming alone. Who cares about getting married anyway? Who wants to have children now? This was what I told myself so that I would accept death...if it ever struck me suddenly.

The moon decided to recognise me finally when I was sitting in church and the faifeau was in the middle of his prayer.

'Bless our village. Bless every household in this our humble village. Bless our beloved country, Samoa. Grant our children wisdom so that they will grow to know you more. Bless also the prayers in the hearts of everyone gathered in your malumalu paia this morning. My voice is but a channel of their humble wishes. Bless all the old in our village. Grant them more days on this earth so that they could further do your work. Bless...'

My crotch was suddenly wet and I felt like I was peeing, but that I would have to sit on the toilet seat for hours to get the pee out. I tried to get Lili and Moa's attention, but their eyes were closed. They too were praying. I stood up quietly to go to the bathroom and check, but Fauakafe slapped my lap.

'Wait till the prayers are over.'

It was the longest prayer I had ever heard. It was the longest church service I had ever attended (besides the fogo i malua services, which dragged on for hours...days...weeks). There was one more song to go before the sege was collected. Then there was another song before the faifeau did his lauga. Then there was one more song before the service ended. The wetness was spreading to my thigh now, and I saw blood on my only Sunday dress. Fauakafe, who was the leader of the altos and always drooled whenever she sang, saw what was happening and shook her head. 'The moon remembered,' I told her. 'I'm not gonna die.'

GANGS — GIRLS — FISH

We were swimming in the sea one day when the 'Five Boys of Samoa,' Sisifo, Peniamina, Laupulu, Fa'imoto, and Misiafa, appeared on the beach yelling and screaming that we get out.

The 'Five Boys of Samoa' was a gang, one that could never decide on a name. You only needed to know what the newest film on the boards of the Tivoli, Savalalo Grand, or Falekifaga o Saiga was to know what the gang's name was going to be that week or that month—if the movie they saw was really good and they saw it three or twelve times in a row. When *Grease* appeared at the Tivoli, the 'Five Boys of Samoa' called themselves the 'M-Birds' ('M' being the abbreviated form for our village, Malaefou). They also made black their uniform and took their fathers' combs to school. For months the 'M-Birds' roamed Malaefou and Apia with black bandanas around their necks (the closest thing to a leather jacket), chewing gum with perfectly combed hair.

They wondered, however, why girls laughed when they walked by, or why other boys from other villages laughed when they walked by, or why their own relatives laughed and laughed and laughed at the sight of them together walking. Someone was finally kind enough to tell them the truth about the way they walked, which was as if they were carrying sacks of sand in their pants or, worse even, as if they needed to take a dump, all five of them together at the same time.

They dropped the walk, but kept the uniform. After all, there was nothing *wrong* with wearing black. Ninjas wore black; so did spies; so did Bruce Lee and John Travolta especially, who was considered a demi-god because of *Grease* and *Saturday Night Fever.*

To them the movies lied. Bruce Lee was king. Bruce Lee could kick Chuck Norris's behind anytime, anywhere. They all agreed—this after they saw the disappointing end to *Return of the Dragon,* where, after what seems an eternity of kung-fu, Bruce dies and a cat appears, and Chuck Norris leaves the scene alive. Such injustice!

To show their loyalty to Bruce, the once 'M-Birds' changed their name to 'Dragon 5.' The new code of the 'Dragon 5' was that they bowed at each other whenever they met. They dropped the bow after that most embarassing of days when Laupulu and Sisifo were at the Eleele Fou flirting with two girls from St Mary's who returned their white teeth with giggling smiles. To show that they were not average—that they were special—and that, as they were gang members, it did not matter that they were not students of Samoa High School, the two dragons bowed to each other... nearly cracking each other's skulls. A man from Faleolo was exiting the bus when he tripped suddenly onto Sisifo whose head then smashed full speed onto Peniamina's small (X-small) skull.

The girls laughed and laughed. The boys had headaches for the rest of the week and avoided catching the bus at the Eleele Fou.

They still, however, respected kung-fu...and Malaefou teenagers respected them for respecting kung-fu, in spite of the Eleele Fou incident (which was the Number One joke throughout the adult community for weeks). They only changed their name to the 'Bee Gees' three months later.

That day when they appeared on the beach, they were wearing not their black code (it was a Saturday after all: *Saturday Night Fever*), but rather bright lavalava with the same hibiscus pattern and 'Samoa is the Pearl of the Pacific' printed parallel on each end.

They pointed at us the way John Travolta pointed in *Saturday Night Fever* and ordered us to get out of the sea immediately. We had just gotten into the sea and had no immediate intentions of getting out. We ignored them, and continued swimming and dancing and singing as we always did.

'You can sing good enough! You can dance good enough! You can even swim good enough, if you call what you're doing swimming. Now get out!'

> Fia vaai atu e ua e sau.
> Faase'ese'e mai o peau.
> Oute faatali atu.
> Oute faatali se'i e sau.

'On the count of ten, you two. One (all five counting), two, three, four, five...'

> E mamao lo'u nuu ma lo'u 'aiga.
> Lau pele aua le faagalo ita.
> Oute moe i le po.

Oute moe miti i ou foliga.

'Last warning, Moa! You'll be eating stones in the next few minutes if you don't get out of there now!'

Moa sang louder and louder, her voice a stubborn message. 'We are staying. We are not getting out!'

Talofa ia te oe ma lou faamoemoe.
Ua ta fiu e tau faatonu oe.
Ae leai o le sao lea.
Taulelea tautino atu pea…

Dong! Splash! Before we could finish the song, a stone hit Moa on the head and Moa sank into the sea. I rushed over to her when a stone hit my head and I, too, sank into the sea. The sky was raining stones and more stones, and angry voices yelling when we both came back up, Moa coughing, me holding onto my sore head.

'If you want more, then stay in there. Otherwise, get out!'

Why were they so anxious to have us leave? Despite their gang-like ways, they were always able to share the sea with us girls. They kept to their side and we kept to ours.

'Something must be up,' said Moa.

Like, maybe they were telling a new dirty joke (which they whispered in such a way that we could hear it, too—that couldn't be it).

'Maybe they're talking about a girl or girls.'

'Oh, stop being silly, Alofa. They do that in front of us all the time.'

'Maybe they're going to jerk themselves off in broad daylight.'

'Cheeky...very cheeky. But it's possible,' said Moa.

With this conclusion in mind we decided it was a good enough excuse to leave the sea. We could watch them from the beach—that's what we were going to do.

'Stop the stones!' we yelled back in unison. 'We're coming out!'

As we came closer and closer to land, our clothes stuck closer and closer to our bodies.

'Your titties are growing-growing girls,' said Sisifo, with a smile on his big wanting-to-be-a-movie-star ugly face. 'Maybe it's time for you to invest in bras. Ever heard of them, Alofa? They're the things they use to...'

Before he could finish his sentence, I snapped back, 'Your Mama can't even fit into a bra, you pig!'

My words, like a towel, wiped the growing smile off of Sisifo's face.

'They don't make bras for whales!' I said...and ran off.

Laughter. Pause. Laughter again. Big loud laughter and then a gorilla sounding roar.

'Take it back!' he roared again and again. 'Take it back before I hit you in the mouth!'

'Is that a demand of your own or did Bruce Lee say that in a movie?'

Peniamina: 'You leave Bruce out of this you, you, you girl. You're just a bunch of girls, dumb-ignorant girls. What do you know about Bruce Lee? What do you know about monkey-style karate, or snake-style, or cat-style or...'

Moa to the rescue: 'Chicken-style. Bruce Lee is a chicken!

Chuck Norris is king.'

Big pause.

We all looked at Moa—stared at her. How dare she say that? How dare she? That was blasphemy. That was blasphemy of the worst kind. It was worse than saying Jesus aikae ten times or Saumaiafe's name five times.

(You were supposed to be struck down by lightning on the count of twelve Jesus aikaes, which happened once to a boy from Falefa who was a Catholic and said 'Jesus eat shit' after he accidently dropped the statue of Mary carrying Jesus on the cement floor of their sitting room. On the other hand, repeating the name of the aitu Saumaeafe five times would lead to her physical manifestation on the spot—this or the offender would receive a sudden red palm print across her/his face. This I have never seen happen.)

I knew then what Moa must have known also: that she was signing away our death passes and that we were not going to leave without one of us in tears. If she wanted to provoke the 'Five Real Men Wear Black' gang, why do it when none of our relatives was in sight? Besides, why use this insult of insults?

We ourselves were obsessed with karate and went to the Falekifaga o Saiga whenever we sold sea-eggs. We worshipped Bruce Lee...perhaps more so than the boys themselves. For a while there I was confused, real confused...until another insult was thrown from the boys.

'Shut up!' Sisifo yelled at Moa. 'Look who's talking about calling people chicken? You were so ugly that poor Iopu and Salagi didn't know what to name you. They saw a chicken walking outside Mokookua and saw your image reflected in the chicken. That's what Simi told us at the last meeting of the Au A Kama.'

'That's a lie and you know it, you overgrown fool. You can't even spell chicken in palagi.'

'C–H–I–C–K–A–N. What do you think of that, you short ugly girl?'

'Why don't you pick on someone smaller and handsomer than you, like King Kong.'

This last insult brought fire to Sisifo's eyes, who always thought himself the handsomest boy in Malaefou. The closest thing to a movie star, Sisifo, was walking now towards Moa with one hand up in the air, formed in a fist, the other hand holding onto his 'Samoa is the Pearl of the Pacific' lavalava.

Sisifo did look like King Kong…in spite of his illusions, he really did. He was taller than most of the grown men of Malaefou. He even had hair growing out of his ears, which was common among old men but extremely rare among fifteen-year-old boys, let alone grown men. He ate like ten pigs put together also, boasting to be able to eat a three-foot taamu without needing to drink water. And when he did drink water he could gallop a whole five-litre bucket in one gulp.

With these proven statistics in mind, I was willing to take back whatever I said about his Mama, whom we all called Mama. Moa would have too. We knew too much about what happened to Fiafia, the twin-girl who teased him about Tautua's (his father's) limb and got a surprising shock between the ears. Once again, none of Moa's brothers were there. None of my brothers, or cousins, or uncles were there either. There wasn't a single relative in sight. (Where were they when you needed them?) We were completely alone—completely alone and surrounded by five former 'M-Birds,' former 'Dragons Kung-Fu Fighters,' 'Bee Gees,'

'Real Men Wear Black' gang members.

'That being the case, why is Moa suddenly so brave?' I asked myself.

'Go ahead!' Moa snapped back, running towards the government road. 'Run…run. Come and catch me, you big bully!'

Sisifo didn't move. Sisifo didn't say a word. The rest of the boys were suddenly quiet as if someone caught their tongues and fed them to eels.

'What's the matter? Can't run? Can't stand up and fight like the real men you think you are? Real men wear black only at funerals, you chicken shit fools. Ha! Ha! Ha!'

I was getting impatient with Moa's bravery, and I wanted to slap her out of whatever was making her do what she was doing.

'Don't you see it, Alofa?'

'See what?' I yelled back, angry this time.

'They can't harm us. They can't even harm a little avaava—get it?'

And that's when it dawned on me suddenly—the source of Moa's sharpness—and I started laughing and laughing too, this time with more confidence. And Moa joined in, and we were laughing together.

I ran over to her and we stood there at the beach, holding hands like we always did whenever we were happy or winning at lape or igave'a, teasing them as they tried to make their way to the sea, one hand holding onto their lavalava (holding them as far away from their skin as they could), while the other hand shook at us, threatening us.

'We're gonna get you when this is all over!'

At that moment we both turned around, lifted up our skirts,

pulled down our panties…and mooned them before they entered the water.

'There's something for you to dream about,' we shouted in our soprano voices.

'Muli lalafa!' was the organized reply of the 'Real Men Wear Black.'

'I wouldn't go too far out if I were you, Fa'i,' Moa roared back. 'I heard avaava hatch their eggs around this time of year and go out looking for small penises to renourish themselves.'

'Well, it's better than some people who just let it grow and are too cowardly to face a little avaaava bite!' all the boys laughed.

Although we had never seen it—and didn't particularly care to—it was common knowledge that Moa's father, Iopu, was not circumcised. Before we had time to react to this last insult we heard the inevitable.

'Auoi ka fia ola!'

A big splash–splash and all the boys came limbing out of the sea. Two voices were crying-crying, one screaming so loudly that it reminded me of the time Tausi went to New Zealand and I was mourning for days.

'Misiafa is bitten! So is Sisifo! Go get help, Alofa!'

I was about to start running when Moa pulled me back.

'No! Go get help yourselves,' she yelled back. 'We're staying right here, aren't we, Alofa?'

Pulu: 'But they're bleeding. Don't you see it? And none of us can run as fast as you girls.'

'Is that so?' said Moa, giving birth to a small smile that grew into a big smile…then into a big, big laugh.

'Is that so?' she asked, or rather simply said to Pulu who was angry now, his face all red, all red-red like a pregnant hibiscus tree.

'What do you mean, you stupid girl?' was all he could muster from his very very weak mouth, which was usually not so weak.

And Moa replied, feistier than before.

'I meant, stop calling me stupid because I'm not. And answer me this one simple question.' A sinister smile shone between Moa's teeth when she said the words 'one simple question.'

'Alofa and I would like to know whether or not it was you, Sisifo, who's been spying on us each evening when we take our showers and that you're going to take back what you said about Iopu, in full confession, now...before your penis bleeds to death and you never get to use it. Confess!'

'I'm not confessing. Why should I confess? Who wants to look at you...?' He couldn't finish his sentence. He was sweating on the forehead and the rest of the boys had sat down on the sand, either too weak or, in Misiafa's case, in too much in pain to move.

After what seemed a silent eternity, Sisifo finally said: 'I only did it once, maybe twice. But I wasn't alone. Peni was with me, too.'

He was worried more then about his penis than about confessing in front of Peni. And Peni, who always held a good fight but whose eyes were now closed and was not reacting in the slightest, let Sisifo spit the words out as if he was re-telling with illustrations parts from *Return of the Dragon*.

We girls all knew of Sisifo's maka-aiku tendencies. Which ranked him the youngest expert maka-aiku in Malaefou—meaning, he had the trained eyes of a ghost. It was his hobby to use his ghost-eyes to spy on girls...and a few women, according to rumour.

And I felt sorry for him somehow…and embarrassed, too, at the same time. What right did we have to force a confession out of him when he was in obvious pain? With this thought in mind I started towards the village, screaming at the top of my lungs. 'Help! Help! Sisifo and Misiafa are bitten! Help!'

Instead of every male rushing down to the beach to save Sisifo and Misiafa, there was laughter from nearly every household as they heard my voice.

'Let them learn to be men!' was the response, said with the enthusiasm of a stuffed dog.

'Make ai!' said Fiafia, the twin-girl. 'Is Sisifo's completely bitten off?'

She laughed and laughed. Everyone understood her joy at Sisifo's pain. Boys are always beating her up because of her big mouth and her tendency to cry at any little thing, like a stone, or hearing someone return her own words.

In general, boys didn't talk to us and we didn't talk back to them. They teased us and we teased back; made fun of us and we made fun of them; ordered us around and we closed our ears to them; winked at us secretly in church during prayer which none of us dared to do back.

But from that day on Sisifo and Misiafa stopped winking at me, stopped making fun of my developing body, the lafa on my neck, my supposed affair with Vikale the fool of Apia…

Instead they started talking to me (but not to Moa), asking me always how I was, how school was, did I need this, did I need that, anything. Moa saw it as a sign that they wanted me to not tell anyone about Sisifo's maka-aiku confession, or worse, that they both had the hots for me and were wooing me at the same time. I saw it differently, much more differently. I saw it as a strange gang code for saying 'fa'afetai,' 'thank you' for the Samoan oil that killed the avaava bite on their penises which somehow turned them into real men, real men who wore hibiscus patterned 'Samoa is the Pearl of the Pacific' bright-bright homemade ie lavalava.

W E

When I was in Standard Three the American peacecorps, Miss Cunningham, gave the class an essay writing assignment.

Write an essay on one of the following topics:
1. My village.
2. My pet.
3. On my way to School today I saw a...

Half the class wrote on 'My village.' I belonged to the other half who decided to write on topic two, 'My pet.'

'My family has a pet. His name is Piki. Piki is born last week. Piki is white and is black too. He likes eating pegu. My sisters and me loves him. We loves him because he is good. He is a good piki and he likes to play with us. He is a good piki and we going eat him when he grows up.'

'Who does the piggy belong to?' asked Miss Cunningham, as she handed me back my essay.

'He is belongs to me, and to my sisters, and to my brothers, and to my 'aiga. He is our piki,' I replied.

'Oh!' said Miss Cunningham, with a smile on her face and her pimples turning red. 'I thought you were going to write about *your* pet, *your* piggy? Do you have anything else that doesn't belong to your sisters too? Something *very special* that doesn't belong to your brothers? Like your toothbrush here at school with *your* name written on it? You know, no one else is allowed to brush their teeth with *your* toothbrush, because it has *your* name written on it. Do you have something at home that's the same as *your* toothbrush here at school?'

'Yes, Miss Cunningham,' I said proudly. 'I have ten sene. It is hiding in a hole under a rock in the garden. No one knows…only Piki and me.'

—

The next time we had essay writing Miss Cunningham narrowed the range of topics to one. The first time, the whole class had written their essays on 'My village' and 'My pet.' Everyone had avoided writing on 'What I saw on my way to school.' I didn't know then why I didn't choose essay topic three. I knew only that it was hard to witness something—anything—alone.

You were *always* with someone. I didn't go to school alone. I went to school with Moa and five, maybe even ten, other girls at the same time. We all woke up when the sun woke up…rolled our sleeping mats…washed our faces…kae le paepae…put on our school uniforms…ran to the store to buy bread…made tea…

drank tea...carried our books on our right hands while a large piece of buttered bread (with jam, if it was pay day) was attached to our left. We all took the same road to school...rode the same bus...snuck out of the back of the bus to avoid paying bus fare... teased the old fool, Siniva...teased Siniva's dogs...threw stones into the Vaipuga...played a game of hairpins...before we entered the gates of Falelua Primary School.

Nothing was witnessed alone. Nothing was witnessed in the 'I' form—nothing but penises and ghosts.

'I' does not exist, Miss Cunningham. 'I' is 'we'...*always.*

GIRL LESSONS

'I' does not exist.
I am not.
My self belongs not to me because 'I' does not exist.
'I' is always 'we,'
is a part of the 'aiga,
a part of the Au a teine,
a part of the Aufaipese,
a part of the Autalavou,
a part of the Aoga a le Faifeau,
a part of the Aoga Aso Sa,
a part of the Church,
a part of the nu'u,
a part of Samoa.

—

Two women were pulling-pulling each other's hair in the middle
of Apia.
They were vomiting insults into each other's mouths,
kicking each other's stomachs,

kicking each other's ribs,
biting each other's ears
'Ai foi gi Moakaa.'
'Ai fou gi au Aleipaka kao ise umu.'
Each woman did not exist in the eyes of the spectators.
Each woman did not have a name.
She 'was' through her village,
and her village 'was' through her.

—

We girls were never allowed to go anywhere after school besides
heading straight home. Even when I started going to Samoa High
School and had afternoon school or had detention or sports practice, I was expected to be home when everyone else was home.

'How come you're late?'

'What detention?'

'You did what?'

'What did the pisikoa say?'

'Was Moa on detention too?'

'How come Moa's been home two hours earlier?'

'So what if we don't have a clock?'

'I know Moa came home two hours ago.'

'Because I say so.'

'And because one more question out of your mouth and I'll
call the boys to tie you up like a pig and beat the shit out of you.'

'Ua e malamalama i la'u kala?'

—

Girls should come straight home from school, take off their

uniforms and hang the bats out—fa'aea le pepe'a. After this ritual of chasing away the scent of flying foxes from the underarms of our uniforms, we were then supposed to have a little something to eat…a piece of bread with coconut, if there was any bread, or anything else lying around the sefe.

The bell for the Aoga a le Faifeau or pastor's school rang, rang and rang around three in the afternoon which everyone under sixteen had to attend—except for Meleane who is eighteen, and all the mothers call fa'akamakama and kids call ai valea, and will probably be in Vasega Ogo for the rest of her life…for the rest of her life, re–e–eally!

At the fale o le faifeau we were taught by the pastor to read the Bible correctly. That is, with meek and humble voices. We were taught also to recite passages from the Bible, to recite all the books of the Bible, from Creation to Revelation where the dragon with ten heads lived. Children were asked to recite creation again and again.

'O ai na faia oe?' (Who made you?)

'O ai lou fa'aola?' (Who is your savior?)

'Name all the twelve apostles.'

'Which book does one find the wedding in Cana in.'

…and so on.

The pastor's faletua taught us girls how to sew, how to dress, how to behave. Whenever we didn't behave, she would pull our ears or pull our hair or slap our faces…no matter how tall we were, no matter how tall we became.

We were not allowed to laugh too much or too loudly.

We were taught to be meek.

We were taught to be humble, again.

140

We were taught also to offer our seats to anyone older than us, regardless of location—may it be a crowded bus, a crowded public toilet in Apia, a crowded anything.

Don't walk *and* eat.

Only pigs walk and eat.

Only pigs stuff themselves and walk.

Always take a shower twice a day, once when you wake up and once in the evening—and three times when you are sick from the moon.

Never wear the same panty twice when you have the moon sickness.

Never laugh at blind people or deaf people…or palagis.

Never walk around alone at night—only bad girls and teine o le po walk around that late.

Never wear anything exposing your knees.

Never wear pants on the malae or at the pastor's house.

Never wear high heels.

Never wear makeup.

Never go to church without a hat.

Never go bra-less to church.

Never speak with the 'k' in your mouth.

Never pray for yourself—you should pray for the whole village and for the whole of Samoa.

'We' were taught to mimic Jesus Christ in all that he was, so that 'we' too could be good examples of his life.

'We' were young ladies, and 'we' should handle ourselves as such.

Therefore:

'I' am 'We.'
'I' does not exist.

ORIGINS (OF WO−MEN)
AND THE BIRTH OF ALOFA

Before our village was called
Malaefou it used to be Malaefouapili. Malaefouapili was born out
of the mouth of a shell—a sacred shell that was 'sa i le La,' or
sacred to the Sun. It was blown down from the heavens by
Matagi, the god of Wind, who carried it on his toes and dropped
it down-down…past Fiji, who blew it to Touia-o-Futuna…who
blew it further on to the east side of Samoa where it laid for many
moons. Waiting. Waiting.

Malaefouapili became the resting place of Pili on Earth. Pili
the Lizard was the only son of the creator Tagaloaalagi. Pili himself was a god—a god known among winds and waves, and clouds
and fire, and shark and bird and boar as the most powerful of them
all.

Unlike those gods who maintain physical permanence
throughout their lives, Pili had the power to transcend his bodily
appearance, manifesting himself in any state of godliness he
wished. This power was most evident in the way he transformed
himself carelessly from Lizard to Lupe, to Aute, to Matagi, to
Tagata. For Pili was able to manifest the metaphysics of his being

into pure physical form, manifesting love in the form of a pigeon, lust in the heart of a hibiscus, strength in the eye of a wind, or beauty in the form of man. This ability to metamorphosise simultaneously, from concepts to man, to beast, to the elements, was the one and only gift given him by his father, Tagaloaalagi.

To maintain his strength, Pili ate stars, drank oceans, ate planets, drank oceans, ate moons, drank oceans, ate suns...ate, ate, ate...until he could no longer eat. He would crawl down to Earth after each feast—crawl or fly or jump or walk or swim—down to the Lower Heavens, or Lalolagi, where Earth gods met the gods of Heaven. It was the new gathering place, the Malaefou, separate from the Ninth Heaven and the Vanimonimo.

Laueleele the Earth god married Fe'e the Octopus and a daughter was born. Her name was Aolele, 'Wandering Cloud.' The umbilicus was cut with bamboo and buried under a mulberry tree. Water was sent to Earth via the stomachs of the bamboo to wash the baby, to wash the mother and to sustain the mulberry tree. Aolele played under the mulberry tree and made siapo, too...and sewed songs like flowers, stringing one to another and another.

Earth gave birth again, and again, and again to seven sons. They were called Tasi, Lua, Ṭolu, Fa, Lima, Ono, and Fitu. They were to be only for their sister, Aolele. They were to fish eels for her, plant plantations for her, harvest ufi for her, bake the ufi in umu, or cook it with coconut milk for her. They were to climb gatae on her command or pulu on her command. They were to swim to the moana, touch the reefs, and return with eels. They were to build canoes for her, make fale for her. They were to beat their heads with stones or tear their hair out of their heads or weep rivers, if any harm fell upon her. They were also to commit suicide upon her death—their souls consequently deemed unfit to enter Pulotu, banished away to Salefe'e where suicide souls roamed. For suicide souls did not have a home. They roamed and roamed and roamed, haunting their living relatives…haunting-haunting-haunting. Nothing grew out of the soil in which they were buried—nothing because they were not worthy…unworthy of life…worthy only of the permanence of death. Thus the seven brothers guarded their sister not only with the strength of their bodies but also with their very souls, for she was to be the sky of their eyes, the source of their pride, their strength. They were to serve her until their souls were ready to leave their bodies for Pulotu. This was the feagaiga. This was the covenant between themselves and their sister. This was their duty.

The 'Pili' that once combined with 'Malaefou' was removed from the name Malaefouapili when Pili was banished back to the Ninth Heaven by the sons of the Earth. War broke one day when Pili, on one of his visiting malaga to Earth, gazed to the east and saw Aolele swimming in a pool next to the sea. Aolele was incarnate beauty—her eyes darker than lama juice, her lips thick like oars from a war canoe, her breasts firm like the heart of a tanoa, her teeth whiter than virgin siapo, her nose noble, experienced, pre-conditioned for greeting…and to take in all of a stranger's agaga…and to release it only if the stranger had honourable intentions. Her legs were strong too, like pou of a fale. Her feet were strong too, like the foundation of a fale—feet that carried her from land to sea to inland to waterfalls to Malaefou, grounding her to her mother the Earth. Reaching for the Earth, too, was her hair…dark, dark hair that fell down her back. Like fern upon the bark of a tamaligi tree, embracing the tamaligi, was Aolele's hair on her back…slightly touching her mother, Earth.

Pili saw this and saw that it was beauty manifested—*beautiful.* He transformed his lustful self into a red-red hibiscus and attached himself to a branch reflected in the water. Aolele saw the aute and reached out to pick it, stroking its petals, talking to it, too, as if it were human. She attached the aute to her left ear (signifying her taupou status) and returned to the water, splashing-splashing, thinking no more about the redness of the aute.

Pili, sensing Aolele's lack of interest in him, transformed himself into a lupe and flew back to the same branch where Aolele first took notice of his existence. Aolele saw the pigeon, a beautiful white pigeon fluttering its wings in the salt of the breeze. She opened her arms and called to the pigeon, and the pigeon replied:

> Aolele!
> O au o le Lupe oute sau mai i Fiti.
> Sau mai i Fiti.
> Toe sau mai i Fiti.
> O Pili e nofo i le Vanimonimo
> O Pili le Atua e saua tele
> Saua tele—toe saua tele
> E pei o se Matagi e agi i le po
> O lona malosi i o ma o…

Before the lupe could finish his song Aolele called out to him.

'Come sit on the water, for I will greet you before I talk to you any longer.'

The lupe, unaware of Aolele's 'greeting' powers flew over and sat on the water where Aolele was. Aolele bent her head to the water, looked into the eyes of the stranger and started to greet him with her nose. She breathed in—or *tried* to breathe in. That is, she brought her nose in contact with the pigeon's peak and tried to take his agaga in. But, the agaga was heavy.

'How could a bird's soul be so heavy?' she asked herself.

She breathed in again and again, and that is when the bird's feathers started dropping off one by one. And instead of wings, the bird stood there with human arms. Then legs were formed, but the head remained that of a lupe. And the half man–half pigeon lupe was sinking, sinking-sinking to the bottom of the pool, each arm slowly turning into the lizard that he was.

Tasi, Lua, Tolu, Fa, Lima, Ono, and Fitu looked down from the Papasosolo where they were standing and saw at once danger—danger to the eye of the sky, danger to Aolele. Before Pili could complete his metamorphosis, Tasi, Lua, Tolu, Fa, Lima, Ono, and Fitu were already on his head, smashing it with stones while they beat the rest of him with clubs and spears…piercing him, too, with the fins of poisonous fish.

Pili fought back, whipping the men with his lizard tongue, clawing at their eyes with his powerful claws, commanding the wind and waves and hurricanes to destroy his attackers. The wind, however, did not respond. Neither did the waves. Neither did the hurricanes. For the wind was sick, and the waves were asleep, and the hurricanes left for Touia-o-Futuna.

Pili was becoming weak—weakened and angry. The poison from the fish wrapped itself tightly, like afa around a pou, around his heart and his brain. Blood spilled for the first time from his flesh, flowing freely into the sea. Pili saw at last that his power was not strong enough to counteract seven angry-angry brothers, so he pleaded for his agaga. He called out to Aolele to have mercy on him.

> Aolele! O oe o le pele, Aolele!
> Aolele! La'u manamea, Aolele!
> Alofa mai ia Pili.
> Pili ua vaivai ma ua fia moe.
> Ma ua fia moe, Aolele!

Aolele looked at him and suddenly tears were formed in her eyes. The seven brothers saw this and had pity for the Pili—the son of Tagaaloalagi, all beaten up, ready to die. They let Pili go on the condition that he gave up the gift of metamorphosis and that he was never to visit Earth in disguise.

Since then, Pili was banished from the Lalolagi and appears only in his permanent condition as a reptile. When he does appear (which is only rare) the people of Malaefou throw stones at the sight of him, or curse at him, killing him over and over...his blood evident each night when the Sun gives birth to the Moon and the pool of Malaefou turns red, blood red. Only a few human eyes are able to witness this. Only pregnant women and those who are sick from ghosts get to witness this metamorphosis of the Malaefou pool signifying the spilt blood of Pili, the god defeated.

Tasi, Lua, Tolu, Fa, Lima, Ono, and Fitu returned to Pulotu afterwards, their bodies too weak to live after fighting a god, their souls too proud to live in weak bodies. Aolele saw this and granted them their wish—that they might enjoy everlasting life in Pulotu.

Aolele herself became stronger. Her mana was increased due to her brothers' sacrifice for her life. To show alofa for her brothers, Aolele wove and wove sinnet and pola, and chopped wood with stone, and gathered stones, and built seven fale on Malaefou. The seven fale stood in a circle, surrounding Malaefou. She then turned herself into the cloud that she was, and wandered the sky. She is always there, looking over the fale of her seven brothers…looking down, too, to Malaefou. But, she does not rest on Malaefou. In memory of her brothers, she floats…floats only and then leaves, returning only when there is a funeral. That is when a soul of Malaefou returns to Pulotu.

'That is why there are only seven main fale in Malaefou today,' said Siniva. 'And that's why pigeons are not blessed in the love songs of Malaefou. Instead they are hunted and killed, and eaten only by the chiefs of the once resting place of the gods.'

—

I heard the story of Aolele for the first time when I was in the womb, and because of it I willed myself female. Pisa was suspicious of this in the fifth month (when body formation is complete) and fought against it with all her power. She ate oysters alone in the dark, raw fish alone in the dark, pig's feet, lemon leaves, and soap, in the hope that the thing in her would die. For she knew that I, like her, was female. She knew it before I was even born. When the ninth month approached, Pisa stopped eating oysters in the dark. She stopped eating raw fish in the dark. She stopped eating pig's feet, lemon leaves, and soap. She forgot. Forgot that the child growing in her womb had a will, and that it had already willed herself 'female.' She began daring instead. She began to dream.

Pisa dreamt that the seed growing-growing had moulded itself freedom—male freedom. For to bear a male child was the easier way for her to enter the Filiga family...even though Filiga already had a wife (two wives)...even though she knew Filiga would not marry her immediately. Filiga's wife, Logo, bore only daughters—two beautiful daughters who, despite their beauty (that is to Pisa, despite their legitimized beauty), would have all attention taken from them and Logo if they had a brother. Like Vaisola.

Vaisola was Filiga's first wife and big secret which all Malaefou understood and feared. No one utters her name alone in the dark. No one goes near the spot where the breadfruit tree used to grow, but is dead now like Vaisola's dead body and womb. Vaisola's womb was like dead soil; it refused to produce anything. It refused to produce a child. People say that that was Filiga's first and only love, and that it broke his heart that he had to leave her because of her dead womb. She in return knew why Filiga kept leaving the house at nights, returning only to shower and pick up his working clothes. She never asked him where he was the previous night, she never did...as if it were normal practice between a husband and a wife.

She herself left the house forever on a rainy Sunday evening, when the evening meal was over and Filiga was still not home. She had been boiling tea that evening, gathering lemon leaves from the tree that grew next to old man Fialogo's grave. She had cleaned the lemon leaves carefully, washing off the dirt and spiderwebs stuck to them. She had then thrown the lemon leaves into the boiling water, waited a few minutes, then removed the leaves from the water...removing them so that the remaining water would not be bitter. Afterwards she added sugar to the pot, stirred it as if her life depended on it, and then buttered up the bread for evening tea, re-heating food from the morning toana'i if there was any left. After everyone had eaten their pieces of buttered bread, and had their cups of hot lemon tea, and all the dishes and cups and knives were washed, she left the kitchen and headed towards her room—*their* room, although he was hardly there. She gathered all her belongings in a plastic bag—all the things dearest to her: the picture of her father smiling in his Sunday best in front of their house, a hat, a coconut leaf hat she had woven that first week when she was a newlywed and they had gone to the plantation to fetch kau for the Sunday umu. She still kept it as reminder of that time when they loved each other so much, so much that it hurt…and she was dying to be pregnant, dying.

Now she was leaving. She had left—not saying a word to anyone, saying no good-byes, her body found hanging from a breadfruit tree later that evening.

A bird told Pisa about Vaisola. Pisa was an outsider. She couldn't have possibly known. Pisa was not jealous of Vaisola. Not at all. Not in the least (even though she may have been Filiga's greatest love). She only felt sorrow. Sadness. Great sadness. Sadness not so much because of Vaisola's suicide, but because of her dead womb.

'How terrible for her to have had a dead womb…how terrible.'

She, Pisa, felt a kick in her own womb when she said this. Kicking-kicking. Her own baby was kicking her from the inside. What is he thinking? What is he saying? What is he remembering? She was convinced it was a boy.

As Pisa thought these thoughts, she thought too that if she, a nobody in the eyes of the Filiga family (and Malaefou), could give Filiga a son all her problems would be solved. Everyone would pamper her and ask her if she wanted anything from Apia, or if there was a special fish she wanted to eat someone would go out to sea to catch it and bring it back, and boil it with coconut milk and onions, or fry it with onions and cabbage, or beans.

'How thoughtful of you to ask,' she would reply. 'I don't want any fish. I would just like a bottle of coca-cola and a keke pua'a. That's all.'

And someone would rush to Emelio's store to get the bottle of coca-cola, all cold and fizzy, and the keke pua'a, warm and spicy …lovely down her oesophagus.

So it was that Pisa fought with all her might to dream, even in the day, to forget Vaisola's haunting memory…even though she had never met her. Pisa forced dreams into her food, in the water she drank, in the showers she took. She was dreaming always, always dreaming of moulding Filiga's seed into a beautiful baby boy—her own peace.

—

Pisa hated me since the day I screamed to the world that I was female, Aolele, exiting her womb. Tears and tears and tears rolled down her face onto the Motootua National Hospital blue sheets of Room 341. Nurses tried to calm her by telling her that I was a strong healthy girl, the biggest baby they'd ever seen, no doubt the loudest. I had a good set of lungs, they said.

Pisa refused to listen, her face dead of any reaction, as dead as a star mound. She refused to look at me. She refused to produce milk to feed me. When I was pressed upon her breast, she would look out the hospital window forgetting that I was even there. The nurses would find me rolling in my own shit or piss, crying-crying on Pisa's lap.

Pisa had forgotten that I was there. She willed herself to forget. Just as I willed myself female. Because of this she even forgot that she'd given birth already. She kept asking the nurse over and over, 'When am I due? When is my son due?'

Sometimes she yelled out at nights, 'You killed my son! You killed my son!'

Despite her angry state she never once hit me, never slapped me on the face, never pinched my fat thighs, never screamed at me when I cried.

A month after she was released from Motootua she started finally to take notice of the female baby in her lap. She bathed it, fed it, wiped the shit when necessary, wiped the piss when necessary. Everything was done methodically. And because of it I never cried; I was a most silent baby.

Some women said I was a good-good baby, that I didn't tire my mother out, that I was already showing the signs of obedience. I would grow up to be graceful, dignified.

Others saw it as an omen. A silent baby meant trouble. One day I would explode and all the things I never said would be collected and vomited out of my mouth one day.

Pisa didn't care much about women-analysis or non-biblical prophesies. She only saw her own death. For in her own eyes, she was already dead. My birth meant her death, and because of it she refused to name me. I was nameless for the first three months. I was the no-name baby. Openly, people referred to me as 'si mea aulelei' ('poor beautiful thing').

'Such a beautiful baby.'

When night fell or when people were not in the open, they referred to me as 'the bastard,' the little ugly bastard who will grow up to be just like her mother, a family-breaker, a paumu-muku…a no one.

Pisa was more aware of what people said behind closed pola than what they said openly, and because of this she decided to bring me up ugly. I was never to know that I was beautiful. I was made to look ugly, I was dressed ugly, made to feel ugly.

And because of this too, Pisa would never sing to me. She let me cry and cry and cry, until I got tired or bored and stopped. She never whispered in my ears. She never even talked to me. Never told me stories about when she, too, was a little girl…never told me stories about Fiakagaka.

I learned all there was to know about being female from copying the nurses, my cousins, and (ultimately) Moa and Lili. Being female according to Pisa was a curse—her mother's curse, her curse, my curse. Fiakagaka, her own mother, eloped with Sale, Lepeka's husband and neighbour. Pisa was the only child from this short-lived elopement, that ended with Sale realising that Lepeka and their five children (all girl-children) were far more important than a virgin schoolgirl giving birth to yet another girl. Sale decided to go back to Lepeka the day Fiakagaka presented him with the hospital bill.

'I'm never gonna be like Pisa when I grow up. I'm never gonna be like Fiakagaka when I grow up. I'll never even look at men. Men don't exist. They *won't*.'

These were the thoughts that flooded Alofa's mind while she

was still a baby—Alofa, who was made to feel ugly (rolling in her own piss, in her own shit) before she knew of rivers, before she looked into mirrors...before she started dying at nights.

POEM OF THE SEA
& BREAKING BABY PROMISES

The sea is asleep. Shhhhhhhhhhh.
The sea is asleep. Ua sua le kai!
The tide is up—the sea is asleep.
Snoring away.
Snoring-snoring away.

It's been a long day.
A long day of fishermen.
Of fisherwomen.
Of children.
Of men, too.
Men who are not fishermen.
Women who are not fisherwomen.
Marching up and down their fire-boat.
Marching-marching between Apia and Pago.
With big liners, too, that carry lamb chops and coca-cola and
    tinned food from New Zealand to Western Samoa.
Australia to Western Samoa.
Japan to Western Samoa.

Washington to Western Samoa.

'They're gonna build a new house!' they say.
'It's gonna be a monument.
It's gonna be the newest thing in the Pacific.
It's gonna make Samoa the centre of the Pacific.
They're gonna build a mammoth.'

The sea in Malaefou is asleep.
Dreaming even.
The sea is dreaming.
Dreams of fishermen.
Gutting bonito.
Letting the blood flow.
Of fire at nights, illuminating the coast...the low
    tide coast.

Women and children look for sea.
Fugafuga.
Kuikui.
And the occasional octopus travelling their way.

Men, strong men.
Brave men. Not so strong, too.
Not so brave, too.
Out with canoes.
Fire in their hands.
Piercing the hearts of flying fish.
A shark.

A turtle.

A turtle refusing to enter the canoe.

Jumping and kicking and kicking.

Jumping and kicking while waves crash onto the canoe.

Shaking it from side to side.

Samuelu Mapusaga the fisherman is used to this.

Used to this kicking-kicking of sharks (even though they
   have no feet).

This kicking-kicking of turtle (because they have feet).

Samuelu is with his son Samuelu le lua, or Samuelu loga lua,
or Samuelu laikiki, or Samu, or Elu—depending on who's calling
him.

Samu holds up the fire.

He holds up the fire while his father spears sharks.

What is going through his head as he does this?

As he holds the fire?

As he spears the sharks?

Samuelu is dreaming.

Dreaming of his wife Lepeka.

Dreaming of the softness between Lepeka's breasts.

Between Lepeka's lips.

He puts his mouth on one of her breasts, eating it greedily as
if it was a mango. Moving his head down to her belly, down to
the stretch-marked belly—full and voluptuous, fertile.

He kisses each mark with his greedy mouth.

Traces each mark with his greedy tongue.
This was Lupe. This was Fale.
This was Siaosi. This was Eleele.
This was Simaima. This was Loto.
This was Samu. This was Moe.
This was John. This is going to be…

Each mark precious.
Each mark a son or a daughter.
All of his children.
All of them living and healthy, too.

Lepeka looks down at her husband Samuelu and is crying,
    too.
'Why do you cry?' he asked her. 'Why?'
Lepeka looks out to the dark.
Out to the sea.
To the other man riding on a chariot, with horses galloping
    on waves…

And Samuelu.
Samuelu continues the song
The dance of his tongue wiggling in the cave he knew so
    well.

—

'It's a big one!' Elu called out to his father.
'A white shark even!'
Samuelu is woken up from the dream of Lepeka.

Slapped back to reality by the voice of Elu his son.
The waves crashing against the canoe.
And Samuelu orders Elu to hold the light out.
'Hold it up high!'

Samuelu saw the shark.
It wasn't a big shark.
It was smaller than the oar of his canoe.
He played with it.
Calling out to his son, 'Let him circle the canoe until he's
    tired!'

After an hour of circling the flames in Elu's hands, the shark
volunteered his flesh to the fisherman and his son who waited
patiently on the canoe.

They added the shark to the rest of the bonitos and Samuelu
thought once more of the best spot at the fish market where he
could sell his catch.

The money he is collecting to buy a fire-boat.
A fire-boat is better than a paopao.
A fire-boat is faster than a paopao.
It is efficient.
And in the fire-boat, he has no need for fire.
At least in this coconut-leaf state.
He would have a kerosene lamp of course.
Maybe even one with benzine.
And he wouldn't have to go fishing every night.
No, Sir!
He would only need to go out three times a week.

Maybe even twice.

He'll catch all the fish he needs to feed his 'aiga and to sell at the Makeki Fou.

And Elu dreams on, too.

Dreams of the karate movie he saw last week.

Bruce Lee kung-fu.

Jackie Chan kung-fu.

Girls.

Elu is nineteen years old.

He is a prefect and captain of his soccer team at school.

Elu goes to Avele College and helps his father fish at nights—weekend nights, that is.

Elu dreams and dreams about girls.

One girl that is—Alofa.

Alofa Filiga lives three houses away from their house.

Alofa goes to Samoa High School, is seventeen years old, and is sitting the government exam to go to New Zealand, plus the School C exam...and he dreams about her a lot...always.

Always he dreams of her.

When she passes by their house his heart beats and beats.

When she's talking to his sister, Simaima, his heart beats some more.

It beats some more. His heart beats especially when he imagines the two of them seeing each other at night, in the back of blind woman Siniva's toilet—this is perhaps the darkest place in the whole of Malaefou.

That's where Elu wants to loose his wings one day.

—

The sun crawls like an ant into its cave.
Setting behind Fito.
Night is born.

Crickets cry.
Dogs howl.
Cats meow.
Tin dishes fall.
WHAM!

'Makuai e valea kele! Makuai e valea kele!' said Pisa Filiga to her daughter Alofa. 'That's what happens when you're constantly thinking of boys! That's what happens when you're constantly thinking of boys!'

Pisa repeated herself whenever she scolded Alofa.

She repeated all insults.

Making sure her husband heard them.

Making sure the whole 'aiga heard them.

And passersby, too.

This was her way of punishing Alofa.

Insulting her.

So that everyone heard.

So that everyone knew.

Sometimes she did this deliberately.

Did this yelling of insults deliberately...only so that other mothers heard her.

Only so that other mothers heard her and said, 'But, Alofa is such a good girl. I don't know why she's yelling at her.'

Alofa Filiga *was* dreaming of boys.

Alo or Fa, as she is nicknamed affectionately by her grand-mother or little cousins, was thinking a lot about boys.

About a boy. Not Samuelu, the fisherman's son who loves her and loves her, and dreams about her all the time—always.

But about Lealofi!

About Lea.

About Lofi, too, sometimes.

Alofa was dreaming a lot about Lealofi.

Lealofi the piano player.

The smartest boy in Malaefou.

The pastor's son.

'Le-a-lo-fi. What a beautiful name,' she says to herself, rolling it over and over on her tongue, scribbling it too on her note-books, schoolbooks, elbows…everywhere.

'Le-a-lo-fi. What a handsome face,' she would say.

Strong legs.

Strong arms.

Strong…

Alofa was dreaming.

Dreaming-dreaming.

Too much to notice that her tin plate was overflowing with curry.

Too much to notice that her fingers were burning-burning.

'Ouch!' a sensory reminder.

'Ouch!' another one.

Damn you, Lealofi!

Damn you, Lea!

Damn you, Lofi!

What are you doing to me, Lealofi?

Was he thinking about her?

Was he dreaming about her?

Were his fingers also burning because he was thinking-thinking about her?

Was he also being insulted by his mother, because he couldn't see straight because he was thinking about her?

Alofa thought and dreamt some more about her love for the pastor's son.

Oh, how much she loved him.

—

And the night was pregnant, then, with stars. But the moon was lost. Lost between clouds, between mango leaves. A shotgun was heard far away, next to the sad cry of a flying fox screeching-screeching to its death far away. Ants were crawling-crawling in the grass. Grasshoppers were asleep. So were the flies in Siniva's toilet.

And it didn't even smell! They didn't even smell it because he was on her, she on him, him on her. Breathing the Coast soap on her skin, in her hair. Like a lizard he forces his tongue into her mouth. Onto her neck. Her shoulders. Her breasts. He buries his head on her breasts. Buries his nose on her breasts. His hands, too.

'I love you,' says he to her, moaning-moaning to her fingering his hair. Fingers around his curly curly hair. Not hearing him.

Not hearing the rain. Not feeling the rain. When he entered her it was pouring, hard.

—

Alofa woke up from the dream because her mother had thrown a kalo in her face, missing her but hitting Whisky the dog.

Whisky made a sad sound and the elders yelled out.

'Kuli i fafo le maile! Chase the dog out!'

'What are you thinking of, Alofa Filiga?'

'What are you thinking of, Alofa Filiga?'

'Your food is getting cold and you haven't touched a damn thing.'

'Your food is getting cold and you haven't touched a damn thing.'

Alofa did not react to the noises her mother made.

That's how she described them.

Noises.

Pisa made noises.

Loud noises only.

At least that was better than being beaten up.

It was better than having your hair cut, shaved even.

Pisa made noises and thought her daughter was embarrassed by them.

This weapon was better than any beating, she thought.

Alofa was not embarrassed when her mother made noises.

She had learnt to die every time Pisa did.

PENISES, EELS, AND DEATH

I started dying at nights, when I saw my father's penis for the first time. When I saw Filiga's penis, it was not alone…it was not with Pisa.

That day I was sick at school and a lizard was crawling in the inside of my head. It hurted.

'It hurts,' I told Moa. 'I'm gonna go home.'

'You have to tell the Wind.'

I didn't want to tell Mrs Samasoni. Mrs Samasoni was our teacher. We called her a bad wind…a bad wind who blew and blew around you until you were sometimes suffocated.

Afi, the boldest and strongest girl in Standard Four B was transferred to our class because she had pulled Miss Cunningham's hair (before she pushed her into a lemon tree for telling her that she was the boldest girl in Falelua). She fainted when Mrs Samasoni whispered something in her ear. When she regained consciousness she was beaten on the legs with the metric ruler and sent home with a three-week suspension note.

Mrs Samasoni was married to Mr Samasoni who taught PE at Avele College. They were both very 'dedicated' teachers who had

166

no children of their own...only Sina. Sina was adopted from Mr Samasoni's sister, Falelima, who already had six daughters and three sons. Sina went on to Samoa High School, after she graduated from Falelua Primary School.

Mrs Samasoni was tall and thin, and had long arms and big eyes. Dog teeth lived in her mouth, next to a sea-urchin tongue. We, the students of Standard Four C, agreed that she looked like an underfed cow. She was the hungriest cow in the whole of Falelua Primary School. She drank children-tears, ate boy-humiliation, and devoured a girl's pain.

When Lisi came to school one day with painted fingernails, she was made to stand in front of the class with a razor. She was supposed to scratch off the paint with the razor, but she cut her fingers accidently. She cried-cried and the blood ran out of her flesh onto the white in her shirt. And Mrs Samasoni told her that that's what happened to cheeky Samoan girls who wanted to be afakasis.

'You are Samoan,' she hissed. 'And you should act like a Samoan girl.'

In spite of her cut fingers, Lisi was on detention after school that same day. She had to weed fifty vaofefe palagi from the back of Form Two. Vaofefe palagi grew there, wild like eels.

Liars and mouth jumpers or guku oso, too, (those who dared to defend themselves) paid a high and painful price in Mrs Samasoni's class. When Iona didn't bring his Maths homework to school and forgot also to bring a hand-broom for Samoan Day, Mrs Samasoni's sea urchin attacked him after morning assembly.

Although Iona tried to explain to Mrs Samasoni that he did do his homework, but that his older sister, Fau, used his exercise book to start the fire for the evening meal, Mrs Samasoni still reacted with venom.

'How dare your mouth jump back at me? How dare? You are a disgrace to my class,' she hissed at him, 'a disgraceful boy who will get an F on his end of the year report card and will be forced to repeat Standard Four C!'

Upon hearing this Iona tried to swallow his tears before they formed, but the large glass marbles were already rolling down to the mat where he was standing. We all saw this and felt afraid for him.

It was during such times that all the students of Standard Four C came together as if in a 'ula pua or a 'ula teuila. Our sorrow or fear were like flowers in the morning dew. We sewed our sorrow and fear into 'ula, and offered it to the victim for consolation.

Mrs Samasoni was aware of this. She saw it and was proud. She was proud of the fact that she could produce such a beautiful 'ula from such low-life creatures as ourselves. To see how far the 'ula could sustain itself, without withering away or breaking, Mrs Samasoni released the tongues of three hibiscus branches onto Iona. The tongues of the hibiscus wrapped themselves around Iona's legs, biting and sucking. Blood-buds bloomed there, too. Wild around his skinny legs.

Whenever Mrs Samasoni entered the classroom we all had to stand up, hands on our sides or sometimes hands folded, and we would say:

'Good morning, Mrs Samasoni.'

'Good afternoon, Mrs Samasoni.'

'Welcome to the room, Mrs Samasoni.'

'Hope you have a good day, Mrs Samasoni.'

'Hope you choke on your food and die tonight, Mrs Samasoni.'

When Mrs Samasoni was absent (and this was rare) we rejoiced. When she was sick we rejoiced some more. Being sick meant that she was absent not only for a day, but for several days...a week if we were lucky.

But then it was quiet...too quiet...too quiet-quiet and we got bored. We got bored with Miss Cunningham, our substitute, who spoke only English and didn't understand us. Boys made us girls have Miss Cunningham come over to our desk and explain something. While Miss Cunningham bent down to explain it, her pink nipples would be in clear view for everyone to see. Everyone knew Miss Cunningham never wore bras. After several explanations Miss Cunningham gave up and the boys would then say:

'Thank you, Miss Cunningham.'

'We understand, Miss Cunningham.'

Miss Cunningham days made us realise that there was something missing. Was it that we actually missed the Wind...missed the metric ruler...missed detention? Missed Mrs Samasoni, even?

Miss Cunningham was good. Miss Cunningham was an angel. Some of the boys were in love with Miss Cunningham. They wrote love notes for her that were never sent...scribbled her name on their desks...helped her carry anything, even if she didn't need it...brought flowers for her...mangoes for her (which meant they had to wake up at five o'clock in the morning to go out to Siniva's mango tree before the dogs woke...which was risky and something they usually did only for their mothers)...and they did their homework in the neatest handwriting they could muster... just to please her.

Girls only liked her. She never hit us...never sent us to the principal's office...never yelled at us, either. In fact, she was always trying to make us laugh. She did this by having us draw our own faces, our neighbours' faces, and trees, in whatever colours we chose. She also taught palagi songs she knew from when she was a young girl in Oregon. She had us dance in circles to the songs.

'So you're not from Amelika?' we asked her.

'Of course I am. Oregon is a part of the fifty states of the United States of America.'

'Oh!' we said, pretending we understood her.

I didn't know then that Amelika was the United States of America. To my Standard Four C mind America was simply Amelika. I believed Miss Cunningham only because one day she brought to school pictures of her and her family. They had a dog and there was a flag of Amelika on each of her relatives' noses.

Sometimes some of the boys got bored, real bored. They were tired of Miss Cunningham telling them at drawing that whatever they did was right.

'There are no wrong answers in Art,' said Miss Cunningham.

'You should express whatever you're feeling at the time you paint or draw or scribble,' she told us.

The boys and all of us girls were confused with this philosophy. How could something not be wrong, we asked ourselves? Our right-wrong world was questioned then for the first time, and we tried as hard as we could to justify our own beliefs. In doing this, we came to the conclusion that it was Miss Cunningham who was making mistakes, not us. Why was it that Miss Cunningham thought the purple trees we drew were normal? She never once said they were beautiful…like Mrs Samasoni would have. She never once said they were ugly either…like Mrs Samasoni would have. They were simply trees—regardless of the fact that some of us intentionally drew clouds, and when Miss Cunningham asked us what they were, we told her they were trees. Miss Cunningham smiled, the red spots on her face getting redder and redder or, sometimes, whiter and whiter. One could never tell what that meant. Is it because the glasses she wore made her see trees as purple and not green? Is it because the glasses she wore prevented her from seeing colours? Or, worse still, did she really think we were *that* dumb and did not deserve the truth? Or that we did not even deserve love? After all, love meant guidelines and rules and punishment. Miss Cunningham's Art meant no guidelines, no rules, and especially no punishment. For the first time we pondered Mrs Samasoni's role in our lives. Mrs Samasoni punished us when we did not follow the rules…when we did not follow guidelines. Mrs Samasoni cared enough to notice when the rules were being broken.

Some of us—those who got punished badly by the wrath of the Wind—became confused when they re-analysed Mrs Samasoni, and they became even more bored with Miss Cunningham's girl scout songs, or brownie songs, as she explained it. They showed their confusion by either refusing to sing or singing flat over and over. This made the rest of the class angry and there was yelling everywhere, until a loud 'Uma lava otou!' flew out of Miss Cunningham's mouth. When Miss Cunningham was cross she started speaking Samoan to us.

The effect this had on us was the complete opposite of what Miss Cunningham had in mind. Instead of everyone returning to their place quietly, loud laughter broke out...everyone was laughing themselves into tears. Confused, Miss Cunningham would rush out of the room, returning to find the next-door teacher laughing with the girls and boys of our class.

We didn't disrespect Miss Cunningham. We didn't dislike her either. We only thought it funny to hear a pisikoa speak Samoan. After all no palagi spoke Samoan. It was the same as if Viliamu, the fool of Apia, had spoken English. We would all break out in laughter if we heard him try...we always did.

—

The best thing I remember about being in Standard Four was the English Poetry Recital Competition and how Mrs Samasoni lead us to victory that year. Mrs Samasoni was one of the few teachers in the whole of Falelua who spoke English perfectly—this being one of the very few things we, her students, were proud of. It is during this time of the year that other Standard Four students actually envied us for being in Mrs Samasoni's class.

Mrs Samasoni's philosophy was that we should recite 'I Wandered Lonely As A Cloud' by William Wordsworth not only at school, but in our homes. Parents, or older brothers and sisters would play a vital role in preparing us for the competition.

Luckily enough, I had cousins who were in high schools and spoke a little English (our own parents did not). Weeks and weeks of practice turned us into experts of the English poem, and although we didn't understand a word of what we recited, we went around Falelua Primary or in our own villages literally singing:

The Daffodils
by William Wordsworth

I wandered lonely as a cloud
That floats on high o'er vales and hills,
When all at once I saw a crowd,
A host, of golden daffodils;
Beside the lake, beneath the trees,
Fluttering and dancing in the breeze...

'So what's a daffodil, Alofa?' Semisi asked me one day.

Semisi was Mu's older brother. Semisi and Mu went to Leififi Primary School. Leififi was where all afakasi and palagi went. It was where all affluent Samoans went, too. Apparently Semisi's class at Leififi was learning the same poem for their English Poetry Competition, but instead of just reciting it they were actually told what daffodils were. Mrs Samasoni never told us what a daffodil was. None of us had the guts to ever ask her.

'What is a daffodil?' I asked myself.

I didn't want Semisi to win this one. I didn't want Leififi to win this one either. So I thought and thought, until finally I came up with what my head told me a daffodil was.

'It's a dancer isn't it?' I said, with both hands pointing at the sky. 'A daffodil is a dancer that lives in the sky.'

Upon hearing this Semisi roared in laughter. He laughed and laughed, and Mu heard him and came out of their falepalagi. Semisi told Mu what I said and Mu laughed too...and I stood there watching them, their mouths wide open. I knew that I was not stupid. I knew this because I was better at the Aoga a le

173

Faifeau and the Aoga Aso Sa than both Mu and her pig brother put together. It was Falelua Primary School that was the problem, not me. So, I was not so hurt when Semisi ran into the malae shouting.

'A daffodil is a bell that doesn't grow at Falelua Primary School. A daffodil is a bell flower that grows only at Leififi.'

——

Metaphysically we were in love with the idea of Falelua Primary School, and worshipped it in the days before we attended it ourselves. Our parents' memories of their own time there were filled with joy and pain...but joy always. Their nostalgia about the good old days, when they had to carry rocks from the river to form the pa at the gate to FPS, the games of marbles they played at recess, the tricks they played on Mrs Vailoa, how Mrs Vailoa was such a tyrant (one everyone feared), how they were sent to the principal's office, how they received the worst slashes on the backside from the toʻotoʻo of Mr Laulau the principal, how despite all this they were 'joyful.' Joyful because they went to school, to where all Malaefouans went. Joyful because they walked to school together, returned home together...walked to school together, returned home together...

These memories made us, too, fall in love with Falelua Primary School. The romanticism attached to the school by our parents made our nights restless—we couldn't wait to be old enough to attend FPS. We counted days, weeks, months...until the day came when we ourselves were clothed in the red and white uniforms characteristic of Falelua Primary School.

We rode the bus that first day...rode it to and from FPS. Our

174

mothers were there with us, too, to see which class we went into
...to see, too, how joyful we would be in attending their alma
mater. They were pleased when they saw us pleased. They left us
there after the third day, when we got used to the idea of going
to school on our own.

Falelua Primary School, we discovered after the first month,
was not as our parents described it. Falelua Primary School was a
plain school. Ordinary. Nothing special. There was still a romanticism alive in our homes whenever our parents reminisced about
Falelua Primary School. Our own reality, however, made us hate
it. We hated Falelua Primary School and we hated our parents for
sending us there. Our parents continued, however, to be in love
with Falelua Primary School—despite the fact that no papalagis
went there...and no afakasis went there...and not a single rich
Samoan went there, either.

'But how could they?' we would ask ourselves.

Or more critically, why would they? Why would a papalagi
send his son or daughter to Falelua Primary School, where the
success rate of its students was close to nil?...academic success
being measured according to the number of Form Two students
who passed the government exam and made it to Samoa High
School or Avele College or Leulumoega Fou (these being the
epitome of a Samoan quality higher education). Those rare one or
two passing students were *extremely* rare. Incidents of this nature
happened only every third year. The rest of the Form Two students continued on, inevitably, to the equally unfashionable
Vaisina or Papalele high schools.

Our parents were fully aware of these statistics. Aware, too,
that Falelua ranked close to the bottom in other unacademic

endeavors, such as the Independence Day Marching Girls' Competition and the National Primary Schools' Athletics Day.

I suppose for our parents two questions battled in their heads whenever they were made to see Falelua for what it really was. The first question (but where else could we send you?) was perhaps not as important as the second (where else could we afford to send you?). After all Falelua was the cheapest school there was if one had five or fourteen children required by law to go to school. Falelua therefore was not an alternative; it was a way of life and an inextricable part of Malaefou history.

We all went there. Cutting grass on Mondays. Learning ABCs and how to speak English. How to multiply, subtract, add. How to sew a book sack. How to sing palagi songs. How to sing the national anthem. How to march for Independence Day. How to avoid being caned or being sent to the principal's office. How to do this. How to do that.

And our parents would remind us how lucky we really were to be a part of Falelua, which meant being part of a tradition. In describing the pains of FPS, which were actually crucial to the making of a good student, our parents would say:

'You children have it so easy nowadays. In our time every teacher was a tyrant. There was no escape. In our time we had to sit on mats on the floor. We didn't even have desks. We didn't even have a blackboard! There were no Miss Cunninghams. There were no peacecorps!'

Mrs Samasoni was perhaps the best thing (besides peacecorps) our parents would say that ever happened to Falelua Primary. Mrs Samasoni was not only a teacher, she was one of them; with the distinction that she was a success—a Falelua rarity who *did* make it to Leulumoega Fou, continued on at the Teachers' College and was the only one who returned to Falelua to give service. Most of the successes of Falelua went on to Samoa High School or to Avele. They were either employed later on by Public Works or the Department of Agriculture or by the Bank of Western Samoa. A minority were flown to New Zealand or to Australia to further develop their Falelua brains. Some of these brains returned in the form of brown papalagis—ones who thought they knew everything there was to know, sat in government offices, rode government cars, spoke English...and were ashamed...ashamed constantly of the fact that they were once students of Falelua. (This according to our mothers who constantly criticised those in our villages who had government jobs, and spoke English, and ate well during the week.)

But not Sila (Mrs Samasoni). She was a true Falelua graduate. She *returned.*

Some people who knew her saw her return to Falelua as a step down, a disgrace...an escape. An escape from the challenge of an important government position. Graduates of Falelua (who were in the majority) thought her decision to return a most celebrated one...challenging...considerate...one that elevated her to the status of demi-goddess for almost all mothers whose sons or daughters were lucky enough to be in one of her classes.

On the first day of every school year we would come home and our mothers would ask us, 'Who's your teacher this year?'

We bowed our heads and looked at the dirt in our toe nails and replied in low-low voices, 'the Wind.'

'What? You mean you're not in Sila's class?'

'Yes [unfortunately], we are,' we whispered. 'We are in Mrs

Samasoni's class.'

'Malo!' they yelled out, embracing us, hugging us (something they rarely did).

They would then treat us special that first week of school. They bought us new uniforms; washed and starched and ironed the new uniforms; bought new panties (underwears for boys), new slippers (red or white as to match the uniform of FPS), handkerchiefs, rubberbands; combed our hair; braided our hair; had us give flowers or pisupo sandwiches to feed the Wind.

We ourselves were given jam and butter sandwiches, and an extra twenty sene for recess.

According to our mothers, being in Mrs Samasoni's class was something to be proud of, something every student at Falefou should wish for...needed.

—

The day the lizard crawled in my brain was the same day a lizard crawled, too, into Mrs Samasoni's stomach and she had to go home on a half-day. She surprised me and Moa and the whole of Standard Four C by telling me lightly and calmly to go home. No further questions asked.

'Just don't let me hear stories that one Alofa Filiga did not really have a lizard in her head and that she was seen climbing mangoes, swimming in the sea, playing hairpins, etc. Understood?'

Strangely enough, the lizard disappeared from my brain. After I heard the Wind's new song, I no longer wanted to go home. I wanted to stay and hear what everyone was going to be talking about at recess. Alofa is this. Alofa is that. Alofa is the new crowned pet. But I couldn't.

Telling the Wind that the lizard had disappeared suddenly and that I didn't really need to go home was completely out of the question—you just *didn't* do it. You didn't want to be beaten for making up a sickness. You didn't want to be called a liar and weed vaofefe for the rest of the afternoon. You didn't want to dance with the metric ruler. I knew this and Moa knew it, and the whole of Standard Four C knew it, too.

So I left. I put my books under the desk, gathered all my pencils together, dropped them into my school sack and left the classroom...left Falelua. Instead of taking the bus that day, I decided to walk. The clouds in the sky looked pregnant with rain, yet still I decided to walk. I walked past Form Two, past the big rock of Sina, past the Vaipuga River, past the Mormon Church, past the Misiluki's mango tree...I walked, walked, walked. Cars zoomed by. Buses zoomed by...one stopped...I didn't get in. I walked... walked some more. I was nearing the bridge at Vailele when the sky gave out a roar—a familiar cry. The clouds were in labour. The clouds were giving birth.

Rain fell when I reached the bridge. I ran as fast as I could under the bridge-umbrella, my hair, my face and my uniform soaking. The river roared at me. Its mouth was getting bigger and bigger, its stomach browner and browner. Wood and tins and paper and more wood flowed down the stomach of the river. Faster and faster they moved. Faster and faster they ran towards the sea. The rain kept pissing...pissing onto the cement umbrella...pissing onto the fast flowing river. Birds were circling in the sky.

One for sorrow, two for joy,

three for a wish and four for boys.
Five for a letter, six for a kiss,
seven for lucky, eight for...?

Wind. I heard the wind blowing. I felt the wind blowing...
laughing, even. And I recognized it...her. Even though I had
never heard her laugh, it was her voice. It was the Wind, indeed.
It was definitely Mrs Samasoni.

'What was she doing here?' I asked my head.

She was supposed to go home, because a lizard was eating her
stomach. She lived at the opposite end of the river. She was supposed to walk to the top of the river, not to the bottom.

'What was she doing there?' I asked myself again (worried this
time).

Was that only a trick? Did she let me go so that she could follow me, and blow her wrath to suffocate me?

Thoughts and thoughts and more thoughts invaded my head.
Fighting there in my brain were thoughts of me naked...weeding
grass naked the whole day and the sun shining on my naked body,
frying it like palolo in pork lard...and the whole of Falelua
Primary School laughing-laughing-laughing at my poor undevel-
oped female body. More thoughts of me in the front of the class—
me swallowing the tongues of hibiscus branches, and all the girls
and boys of Standard Four C throwing vaofefe palagi into my
eyes.

This last thought won the fight of thoughts in my head and I
was frightened. I was about to leave the bridge-umbrella when the
Wind laughed again. This time she was not alone. Two laughters
were laughing-laughing. The other I recognized immediately. It

was the laugh of Filiga. It was the laugh of the one man, besides Jesus Christ and Bruce Lee, whom I worshipped most.

I ran out of the bridge-umbrella. I ran towards a grove of pawpaw trees. The rain was pissing still…harder this time. From under the pawpaw trees I saw the Wind and Filiga moving under the bridge-umbrella. Filiga tore away at the Wind's uniform. The Wind tore away (expertly) at Filiga's working jeans. Her long black hair fell to her naked back. No panties. No bra. Lavalava dropping onto the wet earth.

Then him eating her legs…his tongue rolling up and down her long legs…crawling up to her thighs…crawling into her thighs…resting there…up to her stomach…resting there…up to her breasts…sucking her breasts…large breasts…large, black nipples…sucking-sucking like a piglet…she, crying, hissing…Wind-hissing…blowing little hurricanes into his ears, through his hair into his eyes.

Then I saw 'it.' Like a new-born fugafuga worshipping pregnant clouds, 'it' surrounded by night. Then the tongue…the sharp tongue shinning like day. Dying, too, reborn. That lizard tongue, now, surrounding the cloud worshipper, the fat fugafuga turned eel. She takes the eel into her mouth, eyes closed, fingers scratching his buttocks…eyes closed still…the eel slipping in and out of her now lizard mouth…him crying…crying-crying.

'You're a bitch. You're a pig. You're a paumuku. You're a dog. Eat me, dog. Eat me, dog. Love me like a…'

—

Rain stopped pissing. Pawpaw leaves attacked my arms my legs and I started scratching. I scratched and scratched, until suddenly

181

one of my legs slipped and I fell face first onto the river's arms. The Wind stopped dancing. Filiga looked at me as if…as if…

'What the hell are you doing here?' he wanted to yell…but he couldn't.

He pushed the Wind off of him, covered himself with her lavalava…the eel dying slowly.

'Don't!' hissed the Wind.

'Don't hurt her,' hissed the Wind, again and again.

I was sinking into the sand…sinking further and further. Before Filiga reached me my agaga was no longer there. She had escaped into the lightness and Filiga found only a body…a cold rained-in body wearing a very wet Falelua Primary School uniform—red skirt, white shirt, no shoes, a sack of pencils, two braids above each unpierced ear.

Empty…cold, empty flesh lacking a living soul.

IN BETWEEN DREAMS

I woke up on a mat on the floor of the falesamoa, and I was covered with a blanket. I had no inflicted wounds on my body, but my body was burning with fever.

According to a story, I ran away from school. It rained. I must have fainted when I reached the bridge. I was found unconscious near the road, soaking wet.

Filiga, looking at a fat mo'o on the ceiling, said, 'Why didn't you catch the bus? Lafo said he stopped the bus twice, but you refused to get in. Why didn't you get in? Why?'

'I didn't have bus fare,' I replied, avoiding contact with his eyes.

Vaiusu, Filiga's sister saved him by saying, 'That girl is lying. We found twenty sene in the pocket of her school uniform.'

Pisa's voice (calm, not excited like Vaiusu's), 'Sila said she ran away from school.'

House voices, 'Beat her up!'

'She's pretending to have a fever so that...'

'She's having an affair with Viliamu.'

Laughter. More laughter. Viliamu, the seventy-year-old fool of Apia who sold yellow, sometimes black bananas to children for coca-cola bottles.

'Slap that lying mouth of hers! Teach her now while she's young…before she gets out of control!'

Voices continued to live, to be born and multiply, forcing tears into my feverish eyes, forcing my voice, too, to be heard by ants only…and the mat, and the blanket…and me.

'I'm gonna kill myself!'

Pushing the blanket away from my legs.

'I'm gonna kill myself,' I sobbed.

Pisa slapped me across the face; she slapped me again and again.

Filiga meanwhile had stepped out of the falesamoa, his food untouched.

—

After the event—for that is how I came to remember the thing I saw—Filiga avoided me. He ignored me and was never to speak to me again directly. Not that he ever did, anyway. He had always used his eyes, a grunt, the belt to speak to me before. To show that he was happy or that he was proud, he would smile that happy smile and squeeze my hand in his palm if I was near him. And he would say to me, in such a voice so that no one else could hear, that I was his daughter, and that he was proud that I came first in the Aoga a le Faifeau Annual Exams or that I delivered my lines without fault on White Sunday. When the faifeau himself acknowledged this same pride in Filiga's presence he would just look to his feet and grunt. And I knew. I knew that he was proud. I knew that I was his daughter. I knew with this single grunt that I was loved...even when I danced with the belt on other occasions.

—

One day when Filiga and Pisa left for a wedding in Aleipaka, we were told not to go to the sea. It was a rainy day. Black clouds hovered over the malae and the sea was hungry and we were hungry back, wanting so much to taste waves, blue and blue. So we rushed out of the house as soon as the bus's tail disappeared, practically flying to the sea we did.

Shock is not a strong enough word to properly describe how we felt when we returned home that day to find Filiga's shoes on the steps of the fale. We ran into the back room without showering, put on our dry clothes and ran back to the front room where we hid our bodies under sheets.

'You weren't here when we arrived. Where were you, Alofa?' Pause.

Filiga always had this habit of asking me. I was the oldest.

'Where were you, Alofa? Answer me!'

I tried opening my mouth, tried to say something, anything so as to avoid that loud voice...so as to avoid the belt, hibiscus branch or...?

'We were helping Moa's mother decorate the church.'
Another pause.

Filiga was looking outside. He didn't look directly at us. He was looking outside to the falling rain.

'Are you telling me that Fiasili has two bodies now, Alofa?'
Silence.

'The other body was with us at the faifeau's house just over an hour ago. Isn't that so Pisa?'

More silence. Complete silence.

'Come to me, Loto!'

Loto was the youngest. She was Filiga's eyes and ears among us girls. She skipped over to the chair where Filiga sat smoking a Marlboro.

'Go get the belt! Faavave!'

Loto returned, still skipping with that stupid smile permanently on her face and the snakeskin belt in her fat fingers.

'Pull up your sleeve and give me your arm, Loto.'

Loto did what she was told, pulling her whole dress off of her head like a little puppy pleasing its master with a new trick. For that is how she was. A puppy. She adored Filiga's attention and did everything in her power to have it…to sustain it. So she threw the dress on to the floor and marched over to Filiga, who was now lighting a second cigarette.

'Come closer.'

Loto was now a foot away from Filiga. Filiga lifted Loto's right arm and smelled her elbow. He smelled the other elbow, tasting Loto's skin. We were all familiar with this test. Why didn't we think of it before we dried ourselves, before we put on our clothes. Before we could contemplate further, the snake-belt had already wrapped itself around our legs with much force. Once. Twice. Ten times each leg.

We were not angry at Filiga when he hit us with the belt. We were angry at ourselves for keeping the salt alive in our skin. We should have taken showers before we dried ourselves. We should have killed the salt then. We should have. We should have. How stupid! How utterly stupid.

Filiga continued to avoid me. Worst of all, he avoided punishing me. I was to do whatever I wanted. I only had to ask Tausi, who already had a soft heart for me and gave to me whatever it was I wanted.

Pisa saw this and was not happy. She shook her head whenever I did something that went unpunished. When Moa and I ate the only remaining evening meal fish head on a Sunday afternoon, before the evening church and before the evening meal, the women of the house did not beat us.

'Wait till Filiga comes home!'

'She's gonna get it when Filiga comes home.'

I never did. I was never punished for eating the fish head. Filiga said he was eating at the house of Matai, which led to an outburst of angry house voices.

'But that was for the laulau!'

Filiga was calm. No reaction.

'Have someone go over to Faamelea and write a can of pisupo for the laulau.'

Nothing further. No screamings. No beatings. Not even a word. Just confused women shaking their heads from side to side, pulling my hair, smashing their knuckles onto my skull.

'What's wrong with that man?' they asked, as they untangled their fingers from my hair...which was in pain and not in pain, too, at the same time.

One day, when I lost the key to the family box on a Saturday evening Lupe was outraged. So were the rest of my sisters and brother, who ran around like chickens yelling.

'What do you think were going to wear to church tomorrow?'

Filiga was calm once more. Silent. It was as if I'd won first prize at the Independence Day Marching Girls' Competition. Filiga ordered Pisa to have someone go over to Iopu's and borrow one of his white iefaikaga for the morning service. The rest of the family had to face humiliation and wear colourful clothes to church on Sunday morning.

'Aren't you going to do something?' Pisa was losing her patience. 'You need to do something. People are starting to talk.'

'Let them think what they want to think. I'll have some boys come over on Monday, and open the box, and have another key made. Understand?'

'I was not talking about the box. I was talking about your daughter.'

'Yes?'

'Alofa. I'm talking about Alofa. You can't do this to me. You can't do this to me. She needs to know that you're her father. She needs to be beaten up for Christ's sake!'

—

Filiga answered Pisa's plea on White Sunday. White Sunday is children's Sunday and children rule for the day. It was on this day that I gave the best performance Malaefou had ever seen of Falagi Le Afafine Le Aoga (the vernacular version of The Prodigal Son).

There was nonstop applause. Tears ran everywhere as I delivered Falagi's apology to Ifo her mother. When I looked up from the floor I saw Tausi in tears. Samuelu's wife was in tears, too… and Pisa, her eyes avoiding mine. Even Moa and Lili and Fiafia and Faanoanoa's faces were wet.

188

After the evening service I was approached by Filiga, my heart beating-beating. And I thought to myself, 'Thank you, Jesus. Thank you for answering my prayers. Thank you for making me Filiga's daughter again.'

Yes, I was going back to being his daughter. He was going to squeeze my fingers in front of the whole congregation. He was going to grunt also when someone acknowledged my performance, how brilliant I was, how the whole thing was a success because of me...

But, this is not how it went. Instead of him squeezing my fingers, instead of him grunting, instead of him standing close to me acknowledging that I was his daughter, he stood away... apart...close enough for me to hear him say, 'Pack your things. You're going to go live with Aunty Sisi.'

Then he bowed his head and left. I stood there, mouth wide open. No tears. Dried face. No tears. Not wanting to believe what I had heard. It wasn't that I didn't want to live at Aunty Sisi—that was, after all, every girl's dream: to live with the only member of our 'aiga who lived in Samoa with a papalagi husband.

Pulu leaves brushed against my face. Salt and fish and sharks danced on my lips, their gills flapping against my eyes. Their teeth attacked my flesh, calling me towards the sea. I looked back at the church. Everyone in white. Laughing, singing, and laughing some more. Children eating lollies. Teasing those without. Girls re-delivering their lines again and again.

And I found my feet moving, moving my agaga towards the sea.

MITI

Leaves talk to me at night, when 'I' exist. They show me their bones and their blood, too. And they ask me to suck the blood from them.

'Suck away the pain, Alofa. Suck away the pain.'

Talie leaves fall when the wind is angry and the moon is asleep too. This is when stars fall and fall into the eyes of blind women, who sleep with their mouths wide open.

Wide open, too, was Siniva's mouth—Siniva who was the teller of fagogo in the village of Malaefou. Siniva, they say, was once the most beautiful woman in Malaefou. She had hair the length of a river. Eyes the colour of lava. She had a large brain, too, for a fourteen year old. And all the men in Malaefou loved her…or rather, were 'in lust' with her.

Siniva was the first from Malaefou to go to New Zealand on a government scholarship. She left while everyone was celebrating independence and returned to Samoa in 1972 with a B.A. and an M.A. in history. No one recognized her.

She was fat, wore an afro, wore no bra…and you could easily see her nipples through the Jimmy Hendrix T-shirt she was wearing. Sandals. Peace earrings. Yin–yang rings. And a cap with a picture of a burning American flag and 'Get out of Vietnam' scribbled under it.

She looked like a hippie. She looked like a real bum in the eyes of everyone when she stepped out of the airplane at Faleolo.

'What have you done to yourself?' the women asked. 'What have you done to our Siniva?'

She told them that she was reincarnated (alive), and that reincarnation was not only Buddhistic but very, very Samoan.

Thus she started missing church. Once. Twice. Months, until she stopped completely. She also went around reminding the aualuma of Tagaloa'alagi and the cosmos of ancient Samoa, and the old religion, too, which taught respect for trees, for birds, for fish, and the moon.

And she started telling everyone, too, that pastors and nuns killed Tagaloa'alagi.

'Jesus Christ is not Samoan, do you understand? Cathedrals and churches are graves, cemeteries. Do you understand?'

Her father beat her up. Her brothers beat her up...bad. The women beat her too, with their words. The whole village was embarrassed by her.

'Welcome to Samoa, anyway!' they said. 'Welcome to Malaefou, dearest daughter.'

Siniva tore up the B.A. certificate. She burned the M.A. in front of her mother's teeth, who upon witnessing this diagnosed ma'i aiku—ghost sickness. Taulaaitu, faipele, and taulasea were called from all over Samoa to find out who the angry ghost was, and to exorcise it from Siniva so that she could use her palagi knowledge to secure a job in the government or private sector.

No answer was given. After many lost iekoga and money, the 'aiga decided to let Siniva be.

'Let her live in the Darkness.'

They felt sorry for her. They were angry with her. Their sorrow and anger hung like a black cloud over Siniva, following her everywhere.

—

After that day Siniva started walking the streets of Apia. She walked barefoot with a lavalava around her waist and her breasts hanging under a shocking pink polyester jacket. She would walk and walk, and whenever she grew tired she would sit under the clock in Apia, and smoke banana leaves and wave at palagis.

'Go back to where you came from, you fucking ghosts! Gauguin is dead! There is no paradise!'

Apia children laughed when they heard her speak English to papalagis.

Palagis were confused when they heard such words—most of them were shocked, shocked that someone recognized them doing what they usually did: Peeping-Tomming for a past, an illusion long dead, long buried in museums of their own making. They were ashamed and looked down, buying ulapule or coconut earrings from an old woman out of guilt.

—

Besides being the village fool Siniva was also a warrior. She was anointed by a bird who flew out of the Lightness and took her in his beak. The bird carried her body to the tears of Apaula. There it told Siniva that she was wasting herself, and that she should live as a memory of those who lived in the Lightness.

Siniva listened and listened, and agreed with the bird. And the bird laid an egg in a nest nearby and ordered Siniva to eat the egg.

'Eat the shell, too, especially,' said the bird.

Siniva tasted mythologies in the shell of the egg. She drank legends, too, in the yolk of the egg…licking fagogo…tasting the adventures of Sina and Tigilau…tasting eels, turtles, owls, sharks, and other war gods worshipped in the Light…worshipped by all of Samoa.

'You are free,' said the bird to Siniva. 'You have remembered, again. Return to Malaefou and live among children. Tell them about us, Siniva. Tell them about our Lightness. Tell them that we are still there, that we live on. Tell them, Siniva. Tell them.'

This Siniva obeyed. But, before she left the pond the bird scratched out her eyes and threw them to a water-eel swimming in the tears of the forgotten light.

And I die on and on, forgetting Pisa's noise, not hearing Pisa's noises. I die on until the first ray of dawn…until the first rooster, waking me out of my death.

—

Agaga is the soul that each man and woman has.

Agaga lives in peoples' bodies.

And leaves the body only when one faints, looses consciousness or dies.

My body dies at nights, when a flying cloud hovers like a war-shell over the malae of Malaefou, covering the footprints of children, covering shadows of dogs, exposing the tails of lost eels.

When my body dies, agaga leaves the 'Made In Taiwan'

cotton sheets (all floral and colourful), the 'Made In China' blue or green or red panties, the white polyester brassiere, and the watch also.

The watch ticks…ticks, ticks still…and it's twelve o'clock, too, at night. Twelve o'clock too. And birds are asleep. And flowers are asleep. And fish are asleep. And leaves are awake, photosynthesising away in the dead of the night. This is when ghosts are born again and again. They roam the village looking for a waking baby, looking for a waking cat. Ghosts eat baby eyes and cat eyes…and dreams, too. Ghosts do.

And 'I'?

'I' become a god…'I' am…'I' exist.

—

A child floats in the darkness, eating the beat of its mother's heart. With each heartbeat the child screams. The child cries in the womb. I am the child. I am the screaming child. I am sucking my thumb in the womb of my mother and my mother is crying too. And it makes me cry, too. Cry, too, I do, when my mother is crying, too. I know she is. I know why she does…sitting there in the ocean…somewhere on a wave…somewhere, as I will remember it.

And she is weaving, weaving a mat on a wave.

And she is dancing, too, on a wave…dancing, too, she does, bloodying waves…bloodying waves, she weaves herself into the waves…weaving-weaving…and I am crying-crying in the womb.

My mother wants to kill me. My mother wants to kill me and eat my eyes. She wants me to be born soon so that she can eat my eyes. She makes me cry…she makes me cry and cry.

—

I was born female...and my mother was lying on a beach...and her head was covered with blood...and an owl was sitting there next to her head, drinking-drinking. My mother had been beating her head with coral to stop the pain of giving birth. Right before dawn she died. But before she did, my mother uttered the name of the owl...and I, too, turned into an owl and flew into the sky. Into the sky I flew and flew...and people saw me and pointed at me...and muttered to themselves, too.

'There goes the White Owl, the Owl of Victory!'

They followed and followed me into war. Into war they went. Into war they marched, with clubs and spears...and chants...and angry hearts, too. With angry hearts, too, they slaughtered men... cutting off their heads...cutting off their arms...their legs...cutting out their stomachs...throwing the parts into a umu, where they were baked and fed to dogs—their bodies not worthy of human consumption.

They were enemy flesh—flesh that had died in a state of fear.

—

Tagata is man...is woman...is the 'wo' in 'man'...is 'wo-man.' Tagata was born from fern...from rotten fern...from worms... from sperms. Tagaloa'alagi was wandering around the galaxies... eating stars and planets...shitting...and fucking and fucking, too. Thus earth was born.

Trees and grass and water grew out of the earth, and they continued growing until they reached the ninth heaven. Tagaloa looked down and saw the growing trees and ordered Tuli his son to go kill them.

When Tuli reached the trees, he found a snake sleeping on a

rock. Tuli woke the snake up and ordered the snake to eat all the trees. The snake obeyed Tuli; the snake was afraid of birds. He ate all the trees. He ate all the grass.

And then Tuli flew down from a cloud and hit the snake with a club.

'I didn't tell you to eat the grass, you fucking snake.'

He hit and hit and hit the snake…until the snake died, and turned into a pile of worms…and ta-gata was born…born out of gata…out of the beating of the snake…born out of Tuli's violence.

—

Salevao, the god of rocks, married the Earth…and the Earth was pregnant. The pregnant earth gave birth to Moa. Moa was female. Motion in the middle of the earth, she was. Moa had a brother, too. The little boy was born also from the Earth. His umbilicus was cut from the Earth with a stone and beaten with a club.

Salevao provided water to wash the babe…the boy…the man. And the water was deemed sacred to Moa.

'Sa ia Moa.'

'Sacred to moa.'

'Sa ia Moa.'

So is 'Samoa.'

—

Samoa floats, too, in the middle of her mother's womb. It floats there, too, in the middle of a vast ocean…so peaceful, so fearful…so angry, too, sometimes. So angry, too, she slaps the floating Samoa with a wave once in a while, guiding hurricanes there, too, once in a while.

Samoa is in the middle of her mother's womb—in the middle of her mother's womb she sings...sings, sings of the goddess Nafanua. Marching into war is Nafanua...Nafanua of Pulotu... Nafanua sitting in Pulotu, home of all dead Samoan souls. Nafanua hears the lament of a man one day climbing a coconut tree. His head facing the ground, he plucks the coconut with his feet. He plucks again and again in pain.

'Why do you not pluck the coconut with your fingers?' asks Nafanua?

'Because I'm not permitted,' replies the man.

'Says who?'

'Says the power that rules,' replied the man.

The ruling power was cruel. The ruling power was cruel. Nafanua gathers the invisible people of Samoa and leads them to war, covering her breasts with coconut leaves to disguise the fact that she is a woman-warrior. She leads Samoa into war and over-throws the oppressive power...cutting their heads off one by one...cooling the hot earth with blood.

'I am a warrior,' sings Nafanua. 'I am a warrior.'

'I am,' sings Alofa.

—

He cools my feet with his eyes...massages my ribs with his eyes...embraces my vagina with his kiss...his tentacles caressing-caressing the blackness in my hair...in my mouth.

This is alofa...this is ofa...this is aloha...this is aroha.

This is how octopuses make love to humans...to warriors only...to war goddesses...physical alofa with a sea-god.

After each war I come here. All bloody and full of wounds,

too, is my body—all weary. I go to the side of the sea and rest there…calling to you, oh great octopus…calling to you, my lover.

—

'Alofa is weak,' I say. 'Alofa is dying. Alofa needs water.'

You crawl out of your coral home…out of the stomach of the sea you crawl, to the surface…avoiding the eyes of seagulls… avoiding the eyes of owls…avoiding the beating hearts of dogs. You come to 'be.'

You come to me…your eyes so beautiful…your mouth so delicious…you, my lover…my alofa…la'u manamea.

Sucking my breasts…my tired-tired breasts…all bloody from the wars with men, you drink from my vagina…my tired-tired vagina, all bloody from the wars with men. You embrace me.

You rock me till the sun comes up…until day is born in the stomachs of roosters.

So is Alofa Filiga's reality…each time her body dies.

BEFORE

I fell into the family/village secret when I was caught once stealing from Siniva's mango tree. Siniva was the village fool. She was blind and was my father's sister... something I never knew, for no one in my family or Malaefou had ever mentioned it before.

Siniva was banned from our 'aiga and Malaefou after she returned from New Zealand, and told everyone that Jesus Christ was not Samoan and that people were living in the darkness. The faifeau said she was pitiful and it was such a waste. Siniva was such a waste, said everyone. They thought her a fool and cut the umbilicus that connected her to her mother, Malaefou.

Siniva left Malaefou for a while, and went to live with other people in other villages who also thought her a fool. She was a silent woman when left alone, and spoke only in the company of children. Eventually Siniva returned to Malaefou, where she lived in the abandoned house of the German man who used to live on the outskirts of our village, right where Malaefou meets with Falesasa. Everyone believed the house was haunted by the skeleton of the dead German, that danced and danced with a helmet on its skull at twelve o'clock, midnight always…and that was where Siniva lived.

She had three cats, a dog and a tamed ve'a. And there was also a pigeon that shat all over the roof of the German house. Siniva talked to all of her animals. She never took showers.

And, she stank like a bad toothache. And all the kids were warned of her and the house.

'Stay away from that bitch!' women would say. 'She'll eat you up if you go near her.'

So no one ever did. No one went near her—only during mango season, or to tease the dog, or to test yourself…if you were brave enough.

—

That day Moa and I decided to skip school and hung out at the market. We were spotted by Peau the bum, who told us that if we didn't give him enough money for a pack of Marlboro he would tell on us. We gave him all we had. He was a pig, a Judas-bum pig, and we hated him. He always seemed to know what we were up to.

Because we did not want to risk being seen again, we decided to go out to the plantation and tease Siniva the blind fool…fat Siniva, with the fat dog and the weird red pigeon and fat cats. All of Malaefou teased her. All of Apia teased her, too. People said she was poisoned in New Zealand and that they used her brain for experiments. Other people said that she was fa'alaukakau by a Fijian man who loved her from a distance, but Siniva did not return his love. Other people said she was afraid of the light and confused it with darkness.

Many other theories floated around Malaefou as to why Siniva became the fool that she was. These were the most popular. Even dogs quoted them to other dogs during fights. But, I knew. I was the only girl who knew that Siniva, the fat village fool, was in reality my aunt.

It happened when Moa and I started throwing stones at the mangoes. Moa would throw, and I would crawl under the barbed wire fence to collect the mangoes. Besides Mr Brown (who is not a Samoan), Siniva was the only person in our village to have a fence around her property. This was very unusual, but because she was a fool everyone understood.

It was while I was under the mango that Lulu the dog jumped at me from nowhere and pulled at my skirt. Moa started running as fast as she could, but I could not. My legs refused to run. I fell onto the ground, Lulu barking as loud as he could. My legs died slowly and I felt a complete darkness. The last thing I remembered was flying above the earth…away from the beds where taro patches slept…away from the smell of pig dogs, pigs…away from the horns of taxis and pick-ups…away from the scent of lemon leaves …away from Malaefou…away from the mouth of the universe.

—

The first thing I saw when I opened my eyes was Samoan tobacco floating-floating around a fue, and a to'oto'o and the tuli—the red tuli sitting on a skull of a pig with blood dripping from its peak. I tried to scream out, but couldn't. I screamed again—no voice.

'Where's my voice?' I demanded.

'Do you know what those are?' a male-sounding female voice asked.

'I'm still asleep…I'm still asleep.'

'Do you know what those are again?'

'This is a dream…I am in a dream.'

'No, you are not,' said the bird, spitting blood onto my forehead. 'No, you are not.'

Siniva the blind fool was sitting on a siapo weaving sinnet. I had never seen anyone sit on siapo before, only at funerals.

'Did someone die? Who died? Who?'

'Do you know what those are, Alofa?'

'I am asleep. You are not here. I am not here.'

'Answer me and stop that nonsense!'

'That is a fue, and that is a to'oto'o, and that is a red tuli, and that is a pig's skull. Can I go home now?'

'Do you know what they mean, Alofa…who they belong to?'

'I don't know. I want to go home.'

'This is wisdom. They belonged to a talking chief. When a talking chief dies, he passes these on to his sons and daughters. He hands on his wisdom through the strength of the to'oto'o and the fue. These were given to my father by my grandfather. My grandfather's father got it through his grandfather.

'His grandfather's father got it from a bird. A pigeon was flying in the sea while your forefather was fishing. The blood of a pig's head surrounded his canoe. He was fishing for eels. He was fishing for sharks, too. He was sitting in the canoe and the night was ablaze…ablaze from the fire of his coconut-leaf torch. Your forefather was about to turn the canoe home when he felt the weight of a shark on the line. He pulled and pulled and pulled, and was shocked when he found a pigeon was caught on the other end of the line.

'"Spare my life," said the pigeon to our father. "Spare my life and I will give you wisdom."

'Our father obeyed the pigeon and the pigeon ate his eyes.

'That's why we live in the light, Alofa. Yes, we live in the light. We are spared of this darkness through the wisdom of the to'oto'o, through the hair of the fue. Through fue hair we breath geneologies, poetry...poetry in the scent of flowers and the moon...poetry in the flow of blood from the heads of enemies, from the mouths of enemies. Guarding lightness, we do...tulafale do. Giving birth, and birth to the light of before...before this darkness fell...before this darkness...before this...before...'

—

Cats meowed, fighting and fighting, clawing the heart of a mouse beating beating. Still, too, was the night, the sea, the mango tree. Then the ve'a squeaked once.

'Aue!' called the voice of the male-female.

'Aue!' she called again.

And I stood up from the mat to find myself alone in the house, the house empty—completely empty. All I saw was a half-eaten breadfruit, two pieces of paper all taped up with 'B.A.' and 'M.A.' written on them in capital letters...and a picture, too. It was a picture of a young woman smiling, shining the most beautiful eyes.

A (BO)RING FOR MISS CUNNINGHAM

I will never talk in class again while Miss Cunningham sits in as substitute.

I will never talk in class again while Miss Cunningham sits in as substitute.

(times 498).

I will never talk in class again while Miss Cunningham explains the circumference of a circle, which I don't know because I wasn't paying attention.

I will never talk in class again while Miss Cunningham explains the circumference of a circle, which I don't know because I wasn't paying attention.

(times 98)

I will never talk in class again while Miss Cunningham is explaining the rules to English grammar, even if I think it's boring.

I will never talk.

I will never talk

in class
again
while Miss Cunning–
ham is
ex–plain–ing
the rules
to English
Gram–mar,
even if
I
think it's bo–
ring.

RAIN

I was transferred to Standard Four A—despite the fact that I was not the best of students. Academically I should have been dropped a class lower to Standard Four D, but how could the principal disagree with such an excellent recommendation from his most prized of teachers? Mrs Samasoni was blessed with a miracle of a son over the following nine and a half months. A sister, Eleele, was added to our own 'aiga over those same following nine and a half months.

He was called Rain. He was Timu. One day in December, five years after Mrs Samasoni's miracle, Pisa went to the lauga kogi of Falelua Primary School. Eleele, my youngest sister, was in the Wind's class. That's when Pisa saw him, Timu. Filiga was there in Timu's face. Timu's face reminded her of the first time she saw Logo's girls.

'Who is this boy?' Pisa asked.

'He is my son,' replied the Wind.

Without warning, Pisa grabbed the Wind by her neck, kicking her in the stomach...kicking her some more. She sank her fingernails into the Wind's face, into her eyes…pulling-pulling at her hair…screaming, too, some more.

'You should be ashamed of yourself! You should be baked in an oven, you animal!'

The Wind was released by several teachers who rushed into the room and pulled the two women apart. Mrs Samasoni limped out of the room with torn dress, torn lip, black eye, and Rain crying.

Pisa was wounded like a wounded pigeon after a hurricane… after a storm.

Pisa, the wounded pigeon, sat down on the cement floor and wept, and wept and wept…

I found myself sitting at a desk at Samoa High School. Samoa High School was one of the most prestigious schools in Samoa—besides Avele College for boys, St Mary's College, St Joseph's College, Chanel, and Leulumoega Fou (which was also a good school, but located so far out that no one wished to go there). I was one of three from our village who passed the national exam for entrance to Samoa High School.

Our first day at the new school was marked by our cutting grass and weeding the gardens. It was a long and rainy Christmas holiday. We saw that in the way the weeds grew.

One of the terrors of attending Samoa High School was that everyone had to speak English. Prefects walked around the grounds writing down the names of those who suddenly switched to Samoan. Those whose names appeared on the list found themselves on detention after school, cutting grass or weeding 40 to 50 vaofefe. I managed somehow to hide that most obvious fact, that I did not know how to speak English. I knew the rules of English grammar and I knew how they were organized on paper. I just didn't have the guts to open my mouth and pronounce the written words...which Miss Gunn, the peacecorps, mistook for stupidity. Miss Gunn always spoke extra slowly to me, insulting me with her speech...which I tried to ignore and be polite about.

No one in my family spoke English. No one in our village spoke English besides the faifeau and Falelima, who is an English teacher at Falelua Primary School and married to her books. Besides, I didn't want the other students from our village to be humiliated just because I, a daughter of Malaefou village, did not know how to pronounce the written English.

One day our teacher, Miss Faafouina, showed us an article from *Time* magazine, an article which was supposed to be about us...one we were supposed to be very interested in. The article was written on Samoa and the 'Mead-Freeman Controversy.' None of us knew what the Mead-Freeman controversy was. None of us knew what the word 'controversy' meant.

Because she spoke so quickly, I did not understand anything in the article. Later on I asked a girl from Malifa to explain to me what Miss Faafouina had talked about in class. This is how she explained it.

Mead was a palagi woman who wrote a book on Samoan girls doing 'it' a lot...and they were loving and loved 'it' too. Freeman was a palagi man who said that Mead, the palagi woman, was wrong about Samoan girls doing 'it' a lot...and that Samoans are jealous, hateful, murderous people who do not know how to do 'it.'

That evening I told Lili and Moa what the girl from Malifa explained to me. Lili looked at me and laughed.

'How do you think she knew?' she said.

'Who? What?' I asked.

'How did the palagi woman know that we do "it" a lot?'

'You do "it" a lot, not *we*,' said Moa to Lili.

'Malo Moa!' I laughed.

'And what about the palagi man?' I asked. 'What about him? How does he know that we...I mean, that people like Lili *don't* do it a lot? Ha!'

'I wouldn't know,' said Moa. 'Maybe he was talking to someone like Fauakafe, who'll be a spinster for the already rest of her life...or to some matai, like your father, who are too embarrassed to tell palagis where their hundreds of children come from.'

'Koe Malo Moa!' said Lili.

'Go eat Laulii's shit,' I said to Moa.

'What else are they telling you at Samoa High School? That a man can fly to the moon and have sex with moon people?'

> Pale pale
> Ku le aiku
> I luma o le kou muafale

WINKING & LIKING & LOVING IT TOO

Because I got the moon sickness late (at sixteen years and eleven months), I lost complete interest in boys and tried to avoid them as much as possible.

When someone winked at me in church, I would tell one of my brothers and who would then talk to the winker and then again to me (with a slap on the face, or a pull of the hair, or a line of questioning) for attracting the winker in the first place.

'What did you do? No one just winks at someone just for nothing. You're too kaukala'ikiki. You should stop hanging around Lili. Lili is not a good influence…. Are you wearing makeup?'

It was a no-win, lose-all situation, and I finally reached the point where I just let winkers wink at me, and looked away whenever they did. Some of the winkers would roll their tongues on the top of their upper lips like the vagina women, and say things like: you want it don't you?…and, I can give it to you any-time…and, I can teach you how to kiss like in the movies…and so on.

One of the winkers was the faifeau's son. Everyone saw the

faifeau's children as their own brothers and sisters. They had given up their own villages to preach the word of god in our village therefore they had chosen (or rather god chose them) to be members of our village's 'aiga. Unlike his brothers, Filemoni and Ioane, Lealofi was a pig—all the girls knew it. He had the habits of a wild boar, said the women in the village who noticed the way Lealofi stuffed food into his mouth.

'How could they teach our children about behaving, when they can't even train their own son to be human,' some blasphemous gossip was heard to say.

Despite his pig-like behavior, Lealofi was a good piano player and a very attractive nineteen-year-old catch. Some of the girls were *extremely* attracted to his pig-like habits and found them *extremely* sexy. They wished *extremely* that he would *extremely* wink at them. These were the same girls who in daylight would openly confess that they found Lealofi's manners disgustingly gross, and that he was revolting, and no one in their right mind would be caught dead with him in public, let alone encourage to advances.

Lealofi started following me at nights after choir practices. He never said anything during the first week. He just stood looking at me walk home. I knew that he was looking at me. During the day or during choir practice he would joke freely with my brothers about girls from other villages, and about cars and the newest movie at the Tivoli. He never gave them any reason to believe that he was following me.

—

One night, I took a shower at the public showers, because Moa's paipa had not worked for weeks. Moa's 'aiga had not payed the water bill and their water was cut until the bill from the last month and current month was paid. This was common knowledge to everyone. Moa's mother, however, told villagers that something was wrong with the pipes. Everyone made her believe that they believed her, but actually, no one did or ever does. Moa's mother was a confirmed liar. Even the faifeau knew this.

I was in the dark, soaping my body and washing my hair, when I caught sight of a pair of eyes shining through the teuila.

'Shhhhhh,' they said. 'Pretend I'm not here.'

'I'm gonna scream if you don't leave!'

'No you won't!' the eyes said. 'Shhhhhh.'

I rinsed myself as quickly as possible and left, knowing that the pair of eyes would be following me.

—

In church I avoided the eyes. On the bus I avoided the eyes. In choir practice I avoided the eyes. I avoided the eyes so much, that sometimes when I was asleep I wished somehow that they were looking...looking at me praying to the moon for the sickness... looking at me when I fell in and out of death...looking...

One night the eyes caught me alone. Moa and Lili had decided to go to the Women's Committee Bingo. I had not sold seaeggs that week, and thus had zero money to my name.

'You can help with my cards,' said Moa.

'I've gotta do some homework for school,' I said.

I walked home alone...past the mango tree...past Faamelea's store. I knew the eyes were following me.

They said, 'Don't walk too fast. I have something for you.'

He wanted to give me something and told me that it was in the pocket of his iefaikaga.

I said, you get it out, but he said he couldn't. His fingers hurt too much from playing the piano. I looked around first to see that no one was looking before I reached into his ie. My hand came into immediate contact with his fully erect penis. Instead of removing my hand, as any good young lady would, I found myself standing there in the middle of the malae holding the faifeau's son's penis, saying something stupid like: 'Are you walking or going by bus tomorrow?'

———

'Did you like it?'

'I've never touched one before.'

'I know. We can meet here again on Monday night if you want.'

'I think we should stop before any of my brothers find out.'

'But I'm the faifeau's son. Aren't you forgetting?'

'What do men do to penises with women?'

'They look with them.'

'Really?'

'Yeah…they do.'

'What else do they do with them?'

'They look some more and some more, and they love, too, with them.'

'They do?'

'*I* would.'

SHAME, SHAME, SHAME

I was never to touch Lealofi's penis again. I was never to look into his eyes and feel anything but shame. Shame, shame, shame is what we both felt the night we were caught, and the weeks and months and years since then.

It was a Saturday night and the Aufaipese was having a dance to raise money for our entrance in the Apia county singing competition, scheduled several months ahead. I was with Moa and her cousin, Pepe. Pepe was a blabbermouth, a faikakala, a giveaway of tales. Everyone knew it.

I should have known better than to meet Lealofi, but with the dance and the excitement everyone felt that evening, I did not think that anyone would notice. We had decided after a brief daytime meeting at the church that we would see each other again at the talie on the beach at Falesasa.

The beach at Falesasa was usually empty at nights. A Catholic nun had died there ten years before. Since then everyone kept seeing her ghost walking the beach with her rosary beads down to her feet and a Bible in her hands. She was sick and didn't want to die in a hospital...so said the note on the jacket of the Bible. I was not afraid of the nun's ghost. We were not Catholics.

Besides, I was with the son of a Protestant faifeau.

—

Everything went as planned. Halfway through the dance I told Moa that I was tired and had to go home. I had a test to study for. I told her to say hello to Lili if she saw her and that we would see each other tomorrow at church.

Lealofi was waiting under the talie. He was naked. His lava-lava was on the ground. He smelled of Coast soap. He led me to the ground and unbuttoned my shirt.

'Wait!' I said.

'Someone might be looking,' I said.

'No one is looking,' his fingers slid into the cups of my bra.

'Ei! Faakali!' my eyes looking-looking for a stirring in the bush or the sound of feet.

Lealofi continued doing what he was doing while my head was in the bush still, listening-listening. Then his mouth was on them, sucking them…sucking them.

'Ei! What are you doing? Stop!'

'Don't you like it, Alofa? Don't you?'

'I just don't want anyone to see us. That's all.'

'Don't you like it?'

'I don't know. Maybe I do. I don't know.'

And he put my hands on his penis.

'Where is it?' I asked.

'Shhhhhhhh. Talk to him, Alofa. Talk to him…'

When Lealofi said this I remembered what Lili said about Mr Brown. I still had not seen a penis, I'd only touched it. But that didn't count. Moa said you had to see it in order for it to count.

'Talk to it, Alofa. You'll see.'

'You mean with my mouth?'

'Yes.'

Lili had never mentioned this practice before...and she told us everything. Before my lips pressed onto what I saw as a worm, Lealofi's penis woke up—straight up, suddenly, as I remembered touching it the other night.

That is when the torch flashed on him. And there was Pepe's father—all six foot, 250 pounds of him.

'Put your clothes on and go home. Now!'

Lealofi had already disappeared into the dark before the last word dropped out of Fiapule's mouth. Pepe appeared out of nowhere and called out

'Paumumuku! Maka i fale!'

Small pebbles and leaves were still in my hair when I arrived home.

—

The next morning was a Sunday and I woke up to my normal Sunday chores without anyone discovering anything about the night before. I knew sooner or later that something bad was going to happen to me—real bad.

Filiga was known in our village as the disciplinarian. His reputation preceded him wherever he went. Parents even sent him their children to be disciplined if they were too slow or too weak themselves. This was how Afi was punished when we hid the magazine in her schoolbag. When Solomona's children were caught playing in the vegetable garden, Filiga ordered all six of them and their friends to line up with their pants to the ground, and he spanked their bottoms hard with dried hibiscus branches. When Tomasi's son, Peni, was caught drinking faamafu and smoking cowshit under the Vaipuga bridge, he was sent to Filiga who tied him up like a pig, and beat him with a belt and electric wire until he could no longer move...and women were crying and crying everywhere.

I knew sooner or later that something bad was going to happen to me, and thus savoured the hours of unknown that blessed me. Every Sunday I woke up at six to the sound of the bell, ring-ring-ringing for family morning worship. This I did in silence with Tausi and Fale and Ina, while the rest of the household was asleep still. After the lotu I would roll my mat, go out to the back house and wake the boys for the umu. Someone would usually be awake already, sorting luau leaves or making fire for the morning tea. I would then head off to the tap, wash my face, brush my teeth (if there was toothpaste; if not, I washed my mouth with my fingers).

The household was fully awake now. The older girls were ordering the little girls to go out in the paepae, and pick all the breadfruit leaves and mango leaves...and not to forget cigarette buds. I would be ironing the boys' shirts, iefaikaga, putting everyone's clothes together for church. I tried to be busy, but the whole time I was waiting. Waiting-waiting for Pepe's father to come through the door any minute. Waiting, too, for Pepe to start singing—singing the songs she loved so dearly, gossip.

Still nothing happened, and I went through Sunday School and the whole day without anything, *anything* happening.

That evening at Bible study someone whispered something

between the pages of my Bible.

'They know. Filiga and Pisa know…and the whole of Malaefou knows about it, too.'

—

Monday morning. Busy-busy getting ready to go to school. I had already put on my Samoa High School uniform, 'o le ala i le pule o le tautua.' Filiga, who never talks to me, said he wanted me to go get the scissors and come over to him. He had something to tell me. I reacted normally—as if he was asking me for a pillow, or a cup of tea, or matches for his Marlboro. I was asking people where the scissors were—knowing, but not wanting to know, what they were meant for.

'Where are the scissors?' I asked Eleele, who poked her tongue out at me

'They're in Lealofi's pants.'

Tears came running down my face when I heard Lealofi's name…running down to my feet.

'Where are the scissors? Where?'

'Why are you crying, Alofa? Why are you crying? You should have cried on Saturday night, when the moon was high and all the good girls were in the dance…where they were supposed to be.'

'Fasi ia malepe! Oki ese lauguku ma le pepelo so'o!'

'Malo Alofa! Kalofa e isi keige o Ofa.'

Voices kept flying to me from all directions, like poisonous fish stinging my flesh.

'Where are the scissors?'

—

Before my hair was cut, before my hair was shaved, I was slapped in the face. Then a belt hit me across the face, too…around the waist, around my legs, around my face again. Fists blew in my eyes and mouth and cheeks, and blood flew out onto the cement floor.

'Ua lava ia,' said Tausi.

'Aua le sooga faia si keige o Alofa,' said Tausi again.

But her words only increased the blows to my body. I had stopped crying then. I refused to cry any longer. No tears. Blood flying everywhere, but no tears.

This angered Filiga more and more, and he shouted that he was going to kill me.

'I'm going to kill you, kill you…'

Iopu and Filisi and Saufoi tore him away from my body. He was sweating…his eyes red like fire…his eyes not meeting mine …afraid, somehow, to meet mine.

As if I was the punisher and he the punished…and he knew it…and I knew it. We both knew it too well. By beating me he was beating himself. Beating the Wind. Beating Mrs Samasoni. Beating the memory of that bridge-umbrella rainy day when I saw him naked—completely naked. And since then he was always naked in my eyes.

I was his daughter—once. And he hated me for that. More so than he hated his own sister, Siniva, whom the family killed by cutting off the umbilicus which connected her to the Filiga 'aiga and Malaefou. Filiga hated me more…hated me for being like him. Would I have turned out differently had I not seen the dance of the eel and the lizard mouth? Would I be more, then, like my mother Pisa?

Or maybe I was Pisa. Yes, maybe I was. I was the daughter of my mother. The daughter of the cycle, too…spinning-spinning over and over and over…

———

To further humiliate me I was forced to go to school with my shaven head two weeks after the wounds on my face healed. Filiga kept shaving my head each time he saw hair growing. This continued for a month, until the faifeau visited our fale one evening with Lealofi and we were shamed together in front of our parents.

Lafoga: 'This is your brother, Alofa. This is your sister, Lealofi.'

We were supposed to repeat what he said to each of us. And then he prayed for the both of us, and for our family, and for our village that Satan would be banished from this, the village of God, and that this should be an example to discourage all future attempts at breaking the laws of the church of God.

To further remember the event, children composed songs and poems. They sang this song at nights in the malae or at days to tease not only me, but all the other children of my 'aiga:

> Tatou te olioli
> e fitu fua o Lealofi
> ao si teine o Alofa
> ua tu ma lomilomi
> ao si teine o Alofa
> ua tu ma sogisogi
> ua tu ma sogisogi
> pe e manogi fua o Lealofi.

REAL LOVE

Being beaten up is alofa—love. Real love. Real love is when children are beaten up bad by their parents. Teach the child while he's a child so that he will know when he becomes a man. This is in the Bible. This, too, is written in the earth of Malaefou. To beat a child is to give her respect, to teach her how to behave, to teach her to be humble, to listen, to obey, to love her.

A parent (a father especially) did not love his children when he let them roam around like animals, doing whatever they pleased without consequence. When Moa told Fauakafe (a member of the Women's Committee and guardian of girls in church during services) to eat shit and that she had no business hitting her in church, people blamed Fiasili, Moa's mother.

'That's where she learns it from!'

'That girl is not taught because her own mother is not taught.'

Malaefou parents were defined by the actions of their children, and children in turn were defined by their parents' wrath.

Or lack thereof.

A WEDDING FOR APPLES

Pisa and Filiga married on a Thursday in church, and no feast was thrown or anything. There was a cricket game going while they signed their names in the book at church. Pisa was wearing green sandals with her Sunday best, which looked strange on a Thursday afternoon.

'Why are they wearing white on a Thursday?' asked the girls.

'I don't know,' I said. 'Something about a wedding.'

I never knew they were not married before—like everyone else's parents, who brag about how big the cake was and how beautiful their mother's dress was, and so on. There were no wedding pictures of Pisa and Filiga in the house. Only the one of Logo and Filiga which is at the bottom of Tausi's box and is half eated by cockroaches and bugs. None with Vaisola, the *other* woman—as everyone referred to her when they talked about her...which never happened.

No one took pictures of Pisa and Filiga that day. No one did. It was just another day. Nothing special. Only that Filiga gave all us kids money to go to the store and buy whatever we wanted. Everyone bought lollies and keke pua'a, and coca-cola, and saved their share for a good kung-fu movie at the Fale Kifaga o Saiga. I bought Wella Apple Shampoo with my share and smelled of apples for the rest of the week.

LIZARDS, LICE & EVERYTHING NICE

Again.
There we were again;
sitting on the stones
of the paepae,
of the little red house there.
There,
behind the Public Toilet,
behind the Pulu,
we sit and sit
weaving fans and stories and things,
eating lice
from each other's hair;
taking the dirt out of our fingernails.
Smelling the dirt, too,
in our toenails.
Painting them red
with Maybelline Lush.
We love this.
Love this so.

Love this sitting there
with wind
blowing-blowing on our lips,
between our toes,
between our armpits, too.
Blow.
Blow gently wind.
A lizard shits on a breadfruit of flies,
shits and more flies.
Fly to the sky!
Fly to the sky!
And return to the ulu,
the ulu.
Stinky and slimy.
Stinky and stinky.
The lizard moves on now,
shits and moves on
annoyed
and jealous, too,
of the blood between our teeth.

———

Filiga and Pisa had a fight last night. Filiga told Pisa, in front of the whole village, to pack her things and go back to Savai'i where she came from. And stop bugging him about the fucking cards and the fucking drinking.

'Don't even think of taking any of the children,' he said.

And Pisa yelled back, louder than him, waking everyone up— Lisi and Mika and Faamasino...Lagoto, Sione, Eleele...Pisa laikiki, Salagi…all the dogs in the neighbourhood…and me. All of us kids and other relatives, too, sleeping there in the front house. The boys were safe, sleeping in the faleo'o.

Even after fifteen years they didn't seem to have lost the poison in the fins of the words they stuck into each other.

Until one of them was tired…and then one of them, usually Pisa, would call out to one of us or to the boys in the backhouse.

'Bring some food! Wake up there and bring some food…and a apafafago to the front here. Quick! Makuai maka valea kele gei kamaiki. Kao i se umu se alelo!'

This happened every time Filiga lost his wages at cards or got pissed with some of the men whose wives and kids experience the sameness of our situation—which happened most fortnights.

—

Pisa was gone now, gone to Apia to the Makeki Fou, talking perhaps to a blue fish or a red one, convincing it to come home with her. She was a good cook, she was.

And we sat on, wove on. We sat there some more, sat there with more lice between our lips, lice and blood and all. As if our lips were pierced by a needle slightly or bitten by a sick mosquito.

'What else happened in the village this week?…Last week?… Last year?…Five years ago?'

Five years ago Filifili, the village genius, was admitted to the psychiatric ward at Motootua National Hospital. Everyone knew this story, even the neighbouring villages. Especially the neighbouring villages, who teased kids from Malaefou to this day, singing:

O e ai kae o Fili.
Ma laga kama'i Pili!

We were five years younger then which meant none of us was a teenager. But, we all knew. We all knew the story of Filifili. Who did not? Our mothers resurrected it over and over, whenever they ran out of stories, whenever the TV was broken, whenever the power was out.

According to our mothers, who all sat together at Sisila's house on Mondays weaving mats or played suipi or lami on Tuesdays at Leiloa's house, wove mats again at the Women's Committe House on Wednesdays, told stories at our house on Thursdays, stayed away from each other on Fridays, went to the Makeki Fou together on Saturdays, cooked food for their families before they went off to worship Jesus Christ on Sundays...

According to our mothers, air escaped into Filifili's brain.

'Ga sao le ea i le ulu o le keige.'

What did that mean we asked ourselves? Was that what happened to someone who got too smart, too clever for her own good? Did her brain cry out for oxygen, and when oxygen entered it, fried the brain until she suffocated or, in this case, was admitted? My whole childhood was lived in the fear of being too smart, too clever.

I suppose I was smart. Miss Cunningham said so at Government School. Which frightened me and gave me nightmares constantly. I would nightmare that I came first at the Aoga a le Faifeau and Sewing School. Air entered my brain as a result and all my hair fell off. I was bald for weeks, months...until the next test came and I made sure I was last in the class. Then my hair slowly grew back.

I nightmared again that I knew all the answers to the riddles Tausi told.

'What is a tree with only one leaf?'

'What does a palagi treasure and a Samoan throw away?'

'What sea animal rhymes with the Tuli?'

'What land animal rhymes with Fe'e?'

Air escaped into my brain and I grew hair all over my face. The hair disappeared only when I wrote the answers on a piece of paper and gave them to Tausi who swallowed it. And then the answers were in her stomach—temporarily, until she shat them all out and they dissolved in the earth, where answers to everything come from and return to.

Despite this, I was afraid still. Afraid to let anyone in the village know that I was 'sm__t.' You never know, you might go to sleep and fall into a dream and forget all your teeth…or air might attack your brain and you might suffocate…or worse even, get admitted.

So I faked it—faked anything that showed the slightest sign that I was smart or, even worse, doomed to intelligence. I faked answers to the Suega a le Faifeau…Suega a le Aso Sa…Government School. I deliberately put down mediocre guesses at things even the faifeau knew I knew.

'Who betrayed Jesus?' he would ask.

'Noah?' I would answer with a straight face, trying hard not to be detected.

'What was given to the Apostles at Pentecost?'

'Fish and bread?'

'Why did Sakalio climb up the tree?'

'Because…because Noah forced him to?'

—

Fili did not get sent by her government to Europe, or to America, or to Australia, or New Zealand even. Her brain was not exported to foreign countries to be further developed. She was a product of the Western Samoa education system...a product of Falelua Primary School...Papalele High School...Aoga a le Faifeau... Aoga Aso Sa...Aoga Suisui.

Her name synonymous with excellence. She was only nine months old when she started talking complete sentences. She knew that God made her and that Jesus was her saviour at one and a half. She read the Pi backwards at one and a half and sang the English alphabet, too, at one and a half. Knew how to print her name at two. Took first prize in whatever she did from age four onwards, whether that be handwriting, sewing, or English. Everyone in our village and the neighbouring village thought she could have easily gotten a scholarship to go to any foreign land she wanted. She could have even gone to the University of the South Pacific in Suva if she wanted to. And if not that, then she could have at least enrolled at Alafua, gotten a job at the Bank of Western Samoa, the Post Office...or married a palagi.

But not Fili. That's not what Fili wanted. She did not want any of that. She just wanted to stay in Samoa and play volleyball, and go to the discos, and dissect mice, and love laughing, and be a Science teacher. That's all.

But was that all? Was that *really* all? A boy was involved.

And that's not all. Rumour had it she forced a miscarriage. She never forgave herself. Never. Even on the eve of that night when they took her to Motootua. She was screaming out Uso-o-

Fiakagaka's name (her mother).

'You killed my baby! Murderer!'

—

Where does Uso-o-Fiakagaka fit in all this? How does Uso-o-Fiakagaka fit in all this?

Fili was in Form Five, the year everyone sits School C, when Fiaoso the pulenuu's son stuck his penis in her vagina.

Nothing would happen.

'I swear,' he said. 'I've done this before.… I mean the boys told me how to do "it." '

This after choir practice one night when all the lights were turned off and they were sitting on old man Mose's grave. Mose, named after the good prophet, who was supposed to know whenever someone in Malaefou was gonna breathe his last breath and die.

Mose, too, who told everyone that he was going to die catching the biggest shark *ever* in Malaefou history. But instead, he got hit by a tourist bus under the clock in Apia, and died instantly. Five German couples and two peacecorps were at his funeral, accompanied by twenty Japanese cameras clicking-clicking throughout. They were sitting on old man Mose's grave, him touching-touching the insides of her thighs.

'It,' the act, is called 'intimate bonding'…'private bonding'…'you never do this in public-or-in-daylight bonding'…'making love'…'winning a virgin'…or simply 'fucking.' 'It' depends on who's doing the defining. To Fili's mind and body 'it' was making love, plus all the other bondings. To Fiaoso's penis, 'it' was winning a virgin or the other. To Malaefou 'it' was maka i fale, pure and simple.

That November, two weeks shy of her seventeenth birthday, Fili felt strange sensations in her abdominals...as if pigs were fighting there. The moon decided not to visit her, which was not unusual. So she let things go...and go...and go until two months passed. Her breasts were getting just a little larger than usual and she started vomiting too in the mornings. Her mother noticed... noticed and knew...noticed and knew, but tried to ignore it at first. Maybe it'll go away. Maybe it'll go away. But it didn't go away. It *didn't*. Her breasts became bigger some more. And the pigs were getting more violent and violent. And she was practically seasick most mornings.

'No, it can't be true,' said Uso-o-Fiakagaka. 'No, not my baby. Not my sikolasipi i Giusila.'

'Not *me*,' cried Uso-o-Fiakagaka.

She started thinking then some more. Think, think, think.

'What am I going to do...? What am I going to do...? What?'

A bird heard her desperate cry and cried back in return.

'What *are* you going to do...? What are you going to do...? What?'

—

Someone was yelling at us before we finished telling the story of Fili.

'Come help with the bags! Pogaua!'

Before we even got to last year's headlines...last week... yesterday.

'Come here!' called Pisa.

Pisa, the woman who gave birth to me and reminded me

every day of my life that it was the worse pregnancy ever. She nearly died. I nearly fucking killed her.

'Come here and carry this home.... Whose stories are you girls telling this time? If any stories return to your mouth, Alofa, I swear, in front of this holy church and all the people listening, I'm gonna stand on your throat and pull your vocal cords out. Understand?'

Children poked their tongues out at me when they heard this covering their faces with their hands.

'Ma si keige o Alofa.'

Boys in Avele College uniforms who were walking on the government road heard my mother and smiled silently...and silently some more. My own friends smiled with their teeth at the Avele Boys, muttering.

'Why does she have to come home right now? Right this moment? Does she have a boy detector on her or what?'

'Your mother is a bitch, Alofa. Such a fucking bitch.'

My mother was a bitch—I knew. She embarrased me in front of everyone. Nothing I did was ever enough. Nothing. When I came in second place at the Aoga Aso Sa (a deliberate attempt on my part not to have my hair or teeth fall out in a dream), she looked at me and spoke with her eyes. In her eye-language only I understood.

'Why are you doing this to me? Speak! Why do you have to embarrass me like this? Is *this* how I get payed for all the eight months I carried you. And my stomach had to be cut open to get you out. And you came out while I bled to death there. Bled to death there. Answer me! Why didn't you come first in your class? Why?'

She never warned me about the moon sickness. I had known all there was to know from the girls.

'Don't use any of my lavalava to do your safe' was all she ever said to me.

Because of what happened to Fili and because of her own elopement, which I had told to me (or thrown at my face by village women whenever they were angry with Pisa), she watched me like an owl, constantly.

'Where have you been...? Who were you with...? Where have you been...? Where?'

—

When the baby came out a lizard on the third month, Fili was sent to Motootua. She was sent to Motootua because air escaped to her brain, not because she had just had a miscarriage forced upon her by a clever mother.

When Fili yelled out, 'You killed my baby! Murderers!' Uso-o-Fiakagaka made everyone believe that *that* was the cry of a sick girl...a girl affected by too much oxygen to the brain. Tears rolled down her eyes and most of the women cried too.

'Such a waste.... Such a waste.... She could have been such a good clerk...a good wife to some papalagi,'

I heard my mother talking to her sister, Agalelei, who spent a week here last week from Savai'i.

She was here asking my father's family if they had koga for her Uncle's funeral, which was given in exchange for ufi, a string of magigi, and a sack of Samoan oranges.

My mother was talking about me. My mother was talking. She was writing to my father's sister Miti in New Zealand. Miti wanted me to come and stay with her after Form Five…maybe get a job at a factory or something.

'I don't know what to do,' said my mother to her sister. 'I want Alofa to go…go and find a life for herself in New Zealand. Maybe she'll find some good man to take care of her. Who knows?'

Tears were in my mother's eyes while she said this—'Who knows?'

She did not see me seeing her cry over me. She did not hear me stepping on lizards when she spoke.

'That girl has my heart, Agalelei. That girl is my heart.'

I

Siniva's body is dead. Siniva's agaga is dead too. Siniva's agaga exists no more—not even metaphysically. Rotting inside the coffin-box is her body and her agaga... rotting with siapo. No more...she is no more. She is gone...gone to Salefe'e...gone to Salefe'e where suicide souls die...

The village of Malaefou does not weep and the village of Malaefou does not mourn. It continues. It continues only with hymn singing and prayers after the conch shell curfew, evening meal, choir practice, *Big Time Wrestling, Charlie's Angels, Six Million Dollar Man.*... It continues as if Siniva never existed, as if she was never a part of Malaefou...the Malaefou she loved so dearly. So dearly that it pained her to see it drowning slowly in what she called Darkness, for that is how she defined Malaefou—and the whole of Samoa—by reversing everying.

'We are *not* living in Lightness,' she would say. 'We are not. Lightness is dead. Lightness died that first day in 1830 when the breakers of the sky entered these shores, forcing us all to forget...to forget...to burn our gods...to kill our gods...to re-define everything, recording history in reverse.

'Now,' says Siniva. 'Is our turn to re-evaluate, re-define, re-member...if we dare. For *this* is Darkness. Everyone is living in Darkness and they don't see it.

'Everyone is blinded,' said Siniva. 'Blinded by too many Bibles. Blinded by too many cathedrals...too many cars...too many faleapa...six million dollar men...too much bullshit. For *that* is how it's all gonna end, man—in shit, man...in Darkness shit. And we are all swimming in it, dancing in it, loving it over and over and over...'

—

They found her body at the moana. Eels were living in her eyes. And she was smiling too. The fishermen who found her were afraid of that smile and said they'd never seen anyone die with such a happy face—even though her eyes were missing.

They all swear that she was smiling. That is the only thing anyone cares to remember about Siniva—village fool Siniva, as they all once called her...and continue to call her when women are brave enough to tell of her suicide.

For that is how she chose it. That is how she *wanted* it. Suicide—it was the only way.

—

'Suicide—it is the only way. For isn't that what we're all slowly doing anyway? Each time a child cries for coca-cola instead of coconut-juice the waves close into our lungs. Each time we choose one car, two cars, three cars over canoes and our own feet, the waves close in further. Further and further each time we open supa-keli...pisupo...elegi instead of fishing nets...raising pigs...

237

growing taro…plantations…taamu…breadfruit. Each time we prefer apples to mangoes…pears to mangoes…strawberries to mangoes. Each time we prefer tin and louvres to thatched roofs. Each time we order fast-fast food we hurry the waves into our lungs. We suffocate ourselves—suffocate our babies and our reefs with each plastic diaper…formula milk…baby powder…bottled babyfood and a nuclear bomb, too, once in a while. Drowning our children with each mushroom cloud, *Love Boat…Fantasy Island…Rambo…*video game…polyester shoes, socks—everything polyester.

'We kill ourselves slowly. Every day, every Sunday. Each prayer to Jesus means a nail in our own coffin. Each time we switch something ON (radio, lamps, TV, ignitions…) means a nail in our coffin.

'And agaga as we once knew it dies in our still biologically functionable bodies, full of junk-food…darkness-food…white-food…death food. For *that* is what we consume on a daily basis. We eat Death and we are eaten by Death, too. Symbiotically we live side by side.

'But are we actually living? Could we actually justify breathing in and out…shitting…breathing in and out…pissing…living? No, we can't. *I* can't. I can not. And because of this I've decided to leave. I'm tired. I'm too tired to be…I'm too tired to be…I'm too tired to…

'Thus waste not a tear for me, Alofa. Don't cry. Leave your tears for the living. Don't cry for the dead—at least not for suicide deads; at least not for me. I know that everyone will soon forget me, that nothing will grow out of the remains of my body or my soul. But it doesn't matter.

'What good does it do to grow again in a place where death roams? Where death lives?

'But tell me this once, my little dreamer, did *I* have a choice? Do *you* have a choice now that your own eyes are opened to the darkness?'

I look away…away from the grave…away from the one stone marked, 'Here lies Siniva Filiga—Daughter of Malaefou… Scholar…Heroine…Traitor…Coward…Chicken shit…Bitch… who drowned herself in the moana…traitor who drowned herself in the moana…coward…chicken shit…bitch who's gonna come back to haunt us.'

After reading Siniva's thoughts I am silenced. Alone. For the first time I am alone. I am alone. I am 'I' in its totality—'I' without 'we'…without Moa, Lili, girls, boys…. I am.

What if there is truth in her observations? Like so many before Siniva, should I too pour kerosene over my body and run towards the sea? Should I too put a rope around my neck and hang from a breadfruit tree, drink weedkiller, or eat wild berries?

As I thought these thoughts the Tuli of Tomorrow flew high up in the sky, a fue tattooed on her wings, a to'oto'o tattooed on her peak. The Tuli called to me, her voice music to my feet, and I began walking…walking-walking…away from Siniva's grave… walking now towards Malaefou, towards the new gathering place where 'we' once belonged.

April–December 1994

THE AUTHOR'S ACKNOWLEDGMENTS

I thank my editor, Tony Murrow, for his dedication to the manuscript. I thank my publisher, Robert Holding, for believing in the manuscript (and for convincing me that it should be published).

I am eternally grateful to everyone involved in *where we once belonged*—the audience who heard it performed, and the friends who read it and gave encouragement in Apia, Leipzig, Honolulu, and Auckland. Fa'afetai tele.

I thank the Center for Pacific Islands Studies at the University of Hawai'i, Manoa in collaboration with the Pacific Islands Development Program at the East-West Center for a residency in the Fall of 1994.

Malo le Tapua'i!
Sia Figiel
July 1996

ABOUT THE AUTHOR

Sia Figiel was born in 1967. Her first book *where we once belonged* won the Commonwealth Writer's Prize Best First Book for the Southeast Asia/South Pacific region. She has traveled extensively in Europe and the Pacific Islands, and has had residencies at the University of Technology in Sydney, the East-West Center in Hawai'i, the Pacific Writing Forum at the University of the South Pacific in Fiji, and Logoipulotu College in Savai'i.

Figiel has been on extensive reading tours; recent travels have taken her to New Zealand, Australia, Hawai'i, Los Angeles, London, and Germany. She is also known as a performance poet and has appeared at several international literary festivals. She has worked at a wide variety of jobs including teaching English, housecleaning, waitressing, and serving as an *au pair* while working on *where we once belonged.* She is also a painter and has exhibited her paintings in Samoa and Germany. She lives in Samoa.

GLOSSARY

afakasi half-caste

agaga the soul

'aiga family, extended family

aitu a spirit or a ghost

aka kankala'ikiki a cheeky laugh

aka kuu vala'au wantonly calling out to men

alofa love

au a keine girl guides

aufaipese choir

aukalavou church youth group

fa'afafige transvestite

fa'afetai thank you

fa'alavelave literally, 'trouble': an event where one has to contribute, for example, towards a wedding or funeral

fagogo a myth, legend, or story that is often told with song

faifeau pastor

faikakala gossiper

faipele clairvoyant; one who sees the past or future using a deck of cards

faipepea someone who stinks like a bat

fale house

falepapalagi a Western-style house

faletua a le faifeau pastor's wife

fiafia happy

fogo a kiakogo deacons' meeting

fuga fuga sea cucumber

galuega work

iefaikaga wrap-around for men with pockets on the side

iekoga fine mat

iesolosolo colorful wrap-around

ipu cup or plate

kaikaipese choir leader

keigefaigaluega house girl

kokoalaisa coco-rice pudding

kou faipopolo you

kua back

kui kui sea urchin

lama to trap someone

laulau le sua a ceremonius occasion

lavalava wrap-around

le kaelea someone who doesn't shower

lemigao having no manners

maka-aika a boy or man who spies on young girls or women

makua old, elder

malae open space in a village for ceremonies

malaga a journey

malo hard

matai a chief

meauli literally 'black thing': to describe a black person

mikamika vale to boast excessively

mosooi a type of yellow fragrant flower

oso a traveler's gifts

paepae stones in front of a Samoan house

palagi white person

pisikoa Peace Corps

puipa (paipa) tap, faucet, shower

pulu banyan tree

pu'nelo (pa'uelo) someone who stinks

su'ifefiloi stringing together flowers; a way of telling a story in linked vignettes

supa keli spaghetti

taulasea traditional healer

taule'ale'a untitled young man

tauluaitu medium for the spirits

taupou ceremonial virgin

vaofefe weed